Vampire
Extraction

A NEW WAY

Steve H Hakes

Books by this author:
Vampire Redemption
Vampire Extraction
Vampire Shadows
Vampire Count
Vampire Grail
Israel's Gone Global
Prayer's Gone Global
Singing's Gone Global
The Word's Gone Global
Revelation's Gone Global
The Father's Gone Global
Revisiting The Pilgrim's Progress
Revisiting The Challenging Counterfeit
Salvation Now and Life Beyond

Vampire Extraction

A New Way

Steve H Hakes

Paperback ISBN: 978-0-9957013-9-7

Hardback ISBN: 979-8-4182968-7-0

Kindle ISBN: 978-0-9957013-8-0

V250813103649:   simbolinian@outlook.com

Thanks to...

- Sheridan Le Fanu's non-lesbian, *Carmilla* (1872)
- Christian songwriter/vampire writer, Sabine Baring-Gould's, *Margery of Quether* (1891)
- Bram Stoker's folk-Catholic, *Dracula* (1897)

One   **High Treason**

"The king must die!" Thus spoke Alvah, son of Nindara. Out of the blue he just blurted it out. Today it was millennia past. To them it was 'today'. Far from the green hills lay a dark cave hidden from human sight, wherein dwelt creatures of the night. Often it echoed only to the sounds of silence, but this night a crystal clear note was heard by the nearby ears of one who had waited long to hear.

Nindara was king of the vampires, a people ancient beyond days even at the rising of Eridu—which would one day be called the world's first city. Within this cradle of civilisation—as some of its people, wishing to forget Aratta, were beginning to call it—lived also Kiskilla. She, once princess of Bulika, knew the grief and shame of filicide festering within her. She could have been daughter to the king, yet by her foolish attempt at prophecy had never made it above the rank of councillor, and another had become daughter.

But for that, Alvah would never have spoken. She and the king were both commonly called diaboloi, but diaboloi were Turannoi, and mostly low level foot soldiers to boot, whereas vampires were Pneumata, creatures created within the universe, not beyond it. Less ancient but less evil, theirs was a high and lonely destiny, and to the diaboloi they were more different than chalk to cheese. As far as sheer thelodynamic power was concerned, why, even the weaker vampires could usually defeat third level diaboloi, the tertiaries of the Necros. And the stronger vampires could usually defeat even second level diaboloi, the dunamoi, princes or princesses of evil.

Not that the kingdoms of Night and of Necros were locked in mortal combat, far from it. Now in his twilight years, Nindara, once the strongest of the vampires of Night, had few concerns. There were the vampires of Dawn, of course, mere minor irritations. Assassinations both sides of that divide took place now and again, but fortunately the two sides rarely got in the way of each other, and neither sought all out war: Night would have won by numbers, but at significant loss. This divide all boiled down to perspectives. From the Dawn's perspective, the Children of Usen were to be befriended or at least unharmed—both the firstborn and the secondborn—because they shared the light of Usen. From the king's perspective, the Children of

Usen were theirs to be bled as stuck pigs, for the Night loved the blood of the children and hated the guts of the father. Occasionally they even took mortal possession of their souls—and why not, pray tell? But blood and soul came easier from the secondborn—the firstborn proved difficult to dominate—so the firstborn seldom became their prey.

It was sad to fall out over humanoids, for whom he had little respect. So far as he knew, of all his subjects only Kiskilla had ever questioned whether Usen's children had any meaning in themselves. She had picked up that strange fantasy even before she had been adopted by the Mesopotamian Guardians Meslamtæa and Ereshkigal, when Inanna was her aunt.[i] Having been harangued out of her heresy, her remaining time with the Guardians had passed without undermining her orthodoxy to vampire creed, without awakening old doubts. Kiskilla!

From a deceased world, theirs was a dying race, dying in numbers and in power. For they had come from the orb of Simboliniad, a crystal planet long vanished into the dust of deep heaven, and they did not multiply, though as spirits incarnated they could produce hybrid offspring—though flesh could give birth to flesh, Pneumata could not give birth to Pneumata.

Nindara could not understand why some of his kind had never bowed the knee to Necuratu of the Necros, that supreme Cosmic Power who inflamed them to feast on man. It was a shame to take opposing sides, further depleting their numbers. But why side with Usen, the very one whose Eighth Law had doomed them to this miserable planet, damned them to frustration? Why side with his children, especially the obtuse human vermin that could seldom spot the difference between vampires and diaboloi; that silly vermin given to name-calling, but seldom understanding names?

Some others called them ekimmu, human shades damned because they had died bad deaths. They said that these ekimmu drank life, not blood, and were doomed to forever wander as gusts of wind, spirits seeking to be at peace. Whether true or false, it was imbecilic to turn around and call them vampires! Is there no difference between Psuchai and Pneumata, a rock and a hard place? And some of them spoke of údugs, as if *they* were vampires. Is there no difference between Powers and Pneumata, no end to human folly? Trying to make sense of things but lacking the key, some of them even believed that ekimmu, 'ghosts', became servant spirits, moving from amateur to professional status, so to speak. Is there no difference between Psuchai and Powers?

The best that you could say about humanity was that the wise among them at least twigged that údugs were Powers, some fallen—the diaboloi—and some unfallen—the divinities. But in all fairness it had to be admitted that, although groping around in the dark, their istari were at least groping for light. Incredibly it was rumoured that Usen planned to select one of the wise for a special training scheme, parochial at first, but with a view to going global at an advanced level, once the basic class had learnt their lessons and prepared a way for invasion, intervention. Could such disturbing rumours in the wind be true? It was well known that Usen claimed to love such vermin, but did he really? After all, what were mere mortals that he should be mindful of them; human beings that he should care for them? Nindara could not figure Usen out.

Now sindeldi were a different kettle of fish, made of sterner stuff and much wiser, even as their life spans were monumentally longer, mountains to the molehill years of the secondborn. Even so sometimes they were satirically called *newborn* instead of *firstborn* by the vampires, who in turn were aged to sindeldi as mountains to molehills. In that the sindeldi had been the pattern for the basic DNA form from which the vampires had moulded their default shape, vampires owed them a debt. But they did not owe them friendship. And the vampires owed humanity a debt—in that to sindeldi they were as cattle to warriors, and allowed the vampires to feast free from any real fight. Humans were slow and weak, easily consumed, and their blood hit the right spot. Vampires were safer sticking to humans, and soon after they were discovered, Nindara had officially forbidden sindeldi from the menu.

Humans! Stupid, weak, pathetic little bipeds! And so incredibly blind to the world of spirits! Still, that blindness helped the vampires to stay under cover. A human is stronger than a pecking chicken, but if farm chickens provide good food then why should a human risk their life to crush a thousand chickens? A vampire is stronger than a human, but if humans provide good food then why should a vampire risk their life to crush a dozen humans? As invisible reapers they simply harvested them at need; if a freshly sacrificed human is handy, so much the better—feast well with discretion, was their motto. As for allowing free range humans, why, both Necuratu of the Dark and Usen the Light, forbade otherwise, so humans were under a general, though not a particular, protection from higher up and from deep Darkness. For his part, Necuratu found the Great Game more fun with humans running wild, thinking themselves free. For his part, Usen declared that he would rather die than enslave his children. Nindara's kingdom knew its place, but life would admittedly be more fun if sindeldi and mankind could be hunted rather than gathered.

On his throne of power, Nindara reflected. Five Ages had passed. The humans had had many successes at civilisations, city states united by language and culture, but great wars and natural catastrophes had wiped out their traces, even their languages became at best a disunited babble. But a civilisation was once more developing, this time among a black headed people beginning to be called Saĝigans— would it outlast that of the ancient Atlanteans, or the Númenóreans of the Second Age?

Unlikely, but the Saĝigans were proving themselves to be good neighbours, in a barbaric kind of way. Why, in trying to treat the divinities with respect, they even made offerings to pacify their wrath, believing that bribes would make or move the divinities to side with them against the diaboloi. They didn't believe that diaboloi would be happy with sacrifices anyway—believing them incapable of having their anger untied. They rather believed that diaboloi—when natural methods to undo their work didn't work—could be chased away by the divinities, forced to return to the netherworld through a rite of exorcism that generously packed them off for the journey with food, drink, and clothes.

Only a few Saĝigans feared that the policy of not treating diaboloi as equals with the divinities had caused the problem of diabolical jealousy in the first place. The humans meant well by their offerings, but truth be told they underestimated the divinities. Firstly, in thinking that they needed buttering up. Secondly, in thinking that they needed sacrifices. And thirdly, in thinking that diaboloi were their overkill servants whom they sent to afflict sinful humanity.

In reality divinities—Powers of Light called by some the Plērōma or the Philikoi—were not angry creatures at heart, and cared passionately for those under their care, but their scope for interaction was limited by Usen. For he treated humans with respect, the respect of allowing them to learn through virtue and vice, and both pain and pleasure proved useful teachers. But the Saĝigans were slow students.

To the unfallen Údugs, obedience was always better than giving them things, and the Saĝigans had yet to learn that lovingly offering themselves was the best of offerings, a sacrifice that could only be learnt through obedience of the heart. At best they were at a toddler stage in spiritual development—growth not as an academic learning module but as an imperative to life. Their lessons came through symbolism, and most of the animal sacrifices (they threw in a human now and again) were put to good use: worshippers saw the animals as food; vampires saw the humans as drink.

The Saĝigans would have been grieved to learn of the latter, but hey, ignorance is bliss. The Saĝigans didn't even know that vampires were not the dreaded diaboloi, knowing nothing of the Dynamic Bubble from which Powers still leaked into the universe, nor of the ancient crystal planet, Simboliniad, where Nindara the king had been among the great. His kingdom in its power and glory was still great, yet he was perched in precarious peace, in ignorance bliss.

"The king must die!" It didn't take a genius to realise that, for if it did, then Alvah would not have spoken. Nindara had adopted him for his power, not his perspicacity, for although Anu was not their natural enemy—his cue was to curb the diaboloi—his kingdom posed a clear and current danger, and the Night Kingdom needed strong leaders. Earth had its hotspots of Light, a constant threat. Anu headed the local Light over Mesopotamia.

Nindara seldom listened to his son, but Shirina as always listened closely to her adopted brother, humouring him at times. She was shrewd. Ages ago she had seen that Alvah was a smart replacement for their father. It was for her cunning that she had been adopted, but Nindara hadn't foreseen that that cunning would be used against him. But then, when he had adopted her, he had been in command of all his faculties, and none would have dared to oppose him. Unknown to him he was no longer so safe.

"Yes of course brother, for now you mention it, I can see it for myself. His head shakes with the palsy of old age, and he dribbles at the mouth. It is time for him to leave his people who live by his word. It is clever of you to see what must be done." She smiled sweetly at Alvah, hiding her true sentiments. She meant of course that because Nindara was losing it, some of their people now died by his word rather than lived by it, and that the time had come for a regime change. She had to reinforce Alvah's revelation, lest he bottle out of it on refection. Indeed she had been slowly turning her brother to that very idea that he believed to be his very own: how the foolish think themselves wise!

And how foolish to wait until Nindara withered to the point of falling witless from his throne! He was already making too many mistakes, risking their concealment. Why, he had been spotted recently with his teeth into the neck of a recently sacrificed woman, and been forced to flee through a labyrinth of mainly dark low-roof passageways, pursued by angry temple guards. Turning into a cul-de-sac his only choice had been flight or fight. He had chosen the former, and when the guards had turned the last corner they had pulled up in perplexity. For the only way out was the only way in, unless one could squeeze through an air-vent in the ceiling. Yet no mortal man could reach it, let alone squeeze into it if they should reach it. Yet he had disappeared.

Was he a divinity that had vanished through thick stone walls? But why would a temple divinity run from temple guards? It was uncanny, was finally put down as an apparition of a diaboloi, and the number of guards was increased in all the temples. There was no telling what trouble he would have stirred up for his people, had he been caught alive and talked under torture. It was high time he met his maker. The king must die.

"But can you kill him, brother, isn't he stronger than you?" asked Shirina sweetly. That was intended to sting Alvah into a positive negative.

"What, stronger than me? Of course not. I could kill him with one arm tied behind my back. I can do it with both hands tied behind my back. You just watch me!" exclaimed Alvah heatedly.

Good, he was prepared for regicide, but she mustn't let him go too far. "Yes, of course you can. Please forgive the fatuity of a foolish female—we often speak without thinking." That would placate him, even if he didn't know what 'fatuity' meant: but with a sister like his he had at least gotten to know the word 'highfalutin', letting her words fly over his head. "But not everyone would be happy to know that you had killed your father the king, my pet." Now that should limit his folly and sound sugar-coated too, yet by 'pet' she meant that that was how she treated him—she held his leash. "I expect you have a plan to have the humans corner and kill him, don't you?" Again she dropped her pet some tasty ideas. "Oh I see" she gleefully exclaimed, clapping her hands, "you plan to tempt him back to the same temple and have me block up that hole. How clever of you." That saved him some brain work and let him feel smart without saying a word.

Together clot and clever contemplated patricide; the led and the leader sketched out their scheme of slaughter. Nindara had been wise to choose Alvah to support him as son. Shirina was wise to choose Alvah to support her as sovereign. In reality she would reign as his faithful sister-queen, the true power behind the throne, power and cunning enthroned. But brute power was the winning ticket. Lusty Alvah would be accepted as Nindara's chosen successor, and he and his sister would select a strong son—perhaps Draven, who was strong and sensible.

Two   LONG LIVE KISKILLA

So the day dawned. Brother and sister had shape-shifted into a master stonemason and apprentice, together blocking up the bolthole that Nindara had used. Shirina had already, in the guise of a wise-woman, warned the high priest that the údug could return the way it had left. Consequently he ordered that that shaft be blocked off. Playing to the fear of the cosmic prophecy, she had also spread some rumours that Hamashiach would soon be born among the Yellow River People. That had gotten Kiskilla out of the way, she who ever sought to slay the one from Usen foretold, and so to save her people.

And while Kiskilla searched far away to slay a newborn king, Shirina took her form, setting up Nindara for the kill. Vampires did not mate with each other, but they could still be attractive to each other, pleasing to eye or mind, or maybe just as the comforting presence of a calm or kindred spirit. Thus Kiskilla had long been the consort of Nindara's dreams, though no longer bearing a royal title. Yet she was his chief counsellor and member of the Great Council, and had privately advised him to relinquish the throne and thus allow the Great Council to appoint a successor. Alas he had heeded her not.

Now she seemingly approached him, asking him to take her to the temple where infants were slated to be sacrificed with the rising of the sun. These were healthy babies—she normally confined her appetite to unhealthy ones—and it was a shame, the false Kiskilla said, not to put their deaths to good use, and would be a delicacy for one who normally gave up the pleasures of life. Might she who usually satisfied her thirst with water, not for once enjoy some wine? Would not Nindara the great king smuggle her in through the secret corridors, and stand guard while she feasted on fresh blood? By her false charms she beguiled the king, and as dusk dawned they had secretly stolen in to the temple's inner sanctum, where a number of infants awaited, blissfully unaware of the coming of day. The king had not told anyone of his clandestine destination. Not a soul knew of Kiskilla's return. His fate was sealed.

"Alarm, alarm!" A new guard had spotted a jewelled talisman dropped outside a door for temple priests only. He had discovered the door unlocked, and with his fellows quietly tracked Nindara and the false

Kiskilla to the *sanctum sanctorum*. Surprised by many guards, Nindara and 'Kiskilla' had fled along the same passageways that Nindara had before, but instead of just following him, Shirina had sped down a side passageway she knew to be safe. He fled down the one he assumed to be safe, only to find his bolthole blocked, and himself cornered. He who could not flee fought, he who could once have slain a thousand with a jawbone of an ass—but now the guards were too many and were well-armed.

One in particular fought with the strength of ten men. He who had slain many was at last slain, the new guard yelling to kill rather than capture this diabolos of the Dark. Nindara was of the fire clan, and so his body, released from his will, faded into a pile of smoke and fume and was no more. They had killed their údug, and as they rejoiced the new guard quietly slipped away from the light of their torches. It was later contended among themselves, that he had really been a coward—more glory for them—and had run away from further temple duties lest diaboloi turned up for revenge.

The following day the babies were sacrificed in honour of the divinity that had overcome the diabolos, and their parents wept. The guards made no mention of the údug that had escaped, nor the guard who had deserted. They were heroes, and preferred not to share their glory with another.

The following day the vampires were in the dark, wondering why their king had so rashly revisited the hornet's nest. With crocodile tears, Alvah and Shirina bewailed their father's fall, and Alvah's enthronement was demanded before the Great Council. But the Great Council was incomplete without Kiskilla, and Rangda was sent to bring her in. Alvah waited long days in trepidation. Like many a fool, only after his folly did he fear the consequences. Shirina refused to discuss the issue with him. Tersely she had told him to keep his mouth shut, not to raise any suspicions, to act as an innocent in mourning.

A full week had gone by, half a blink of an eye to a vampire, but an eternity when one's fate hangs in the balance. Rangda had had problems finding Kiskilla, for as a field operative Kiskilla had been under cover, covering her tracks. Hamashiach had not turned up, and now they were back, and now Kiskilla suspected intrigue.

Questioned, a royal guard admitted that he had had a sneaking suspicion that someone had visited the king shortly before he was killed. Kiskilla personally began to investigate.

Dressed as a temple prostitute she entered the temple and dined with the guards. "Yes lady," she was told, "we found a talisman dropped by the holy door, and then found the evil údug biting an infant neck. We chased it to a dead-end and slew it after a ferocious fight. We lost six guards, but with the divinity's help we had the victory. Lo, its body twisted and burnt before us—and what stench! Not a sight that a pretty woman like you would ever wish to see." And one of the guards took her to where the talisman had been stored. Kiskilla smelt it—she knew that smell—stole it, and stole back to the her cave.

"Long ago our father chose us to be his children. Long has it been our people's tradition that a he should take the throne, and respecting that, I, erstwhile daughter of the departed, do relinquish my claim in favour of my dear brother, dear to me as ever was my father", announced Shirina before the Great Council. "Tradition too has been to enthrone a royal adoptee, therefore I urge you all to enthrone mighty Alvah, he whom none of our people can out-master in battle. Hail Alvah!"

The Great Council looked with favour upon brother and sister. Her words were reasonable, and her words were fair. Many heads sagely nodded in tacit agreement. It was true that Alvah was strong of limb, rather than of mind, yet Nindara had had two children, choosing strength and sense. To enthrone Alvah would be welcome news to the body politic, who idolised brute force, and his queen would surely be his sensible sister, a formidable pair to rule them. Tradition was not enthroned, and others could be considered, but so far none had put forward any other name, and only one other name formed in the minds of the Great Council.

From their number Kiskilla arose. "Shirina" said she sweetly, "your cunning will enrich the skills of your brother, once he takes his throne, and will no doubt enrich us all. Alas your late father had lost somewhat his cunning, for which I had urged him to relinquish his throne, but foolishly he would not. And foolish perhaps that he rashly returned to a temple from which he had earlier escaped by the skin of his teeth. But no more foolish than its guards, whom I have twice met. The first time, well.... But the second time wine loosened their lips, and they spoke of two intruders, and of the king being cornered in a place where an unknown wise-woman had counselled them to block up any escape—for the king had fled that same way before. Who was that wise-woman, I wonder? And the sacrifices were to be of infants. Not the king's tipple, I think. Did he go to escort another, perhaps, some favourite of his? And it was a new temple guard who found signs of intruders, and also ensured the king's death, then mysteriously disappeared without trace. Well well, the king's death is shrouded in mystery, isn't it. How unfortunate that I was away, following rumours, rumours now seeming false, for otherwise I might have been with the king when his guards suspected that someone had snuck in. I wonder who started those rumours that led me away. Shirina, where is your talisman? High treason!" she shouted, holding up the talisman, "this was found by the unknown temple guard. Shirina has betrayed he who was her father the king. And who came among the human guards but her brother? Has his strong arm not slain the king?"

The secret was out. Betrayed, betrayed by her bungling fool of a brother. She had told him to keep hold of the talisman. Instead he had meekly given it to the ugula of the guard when asked. At least in the fray he should have killed the ugula and taken back the talisman. That she herself could have planted something untraceable at that doorway, she didn't like to remind herself, nor had she time to before council guards took hold of them both. The game was up. Their fate was sealed. The evidence was out, both circumstantial and hard. Kiskilla's honesty was known and admired by the council, who played by the rule that takiya—the law of untruth—only condoned, at times commended, lying to those outside the circle.

By order of Gjaku, they who had been Nindara's children were taken away from the council for summary execution, royal flames to be extinguished. The body of Alvah would soon corrupt, for he was of the water clan, and soon he would be released unto Usen for the final judgement. The body of Shirina would conserve, for she was of the ice clan, yet her body would be hidden and entombed beyond her sight, and she would flit unseen, unheard, untouched, endlessly searching but never finding, released to her final fate only when her uncorrupt body was finally destroyed, perhaps by the unmaking of Middle-earth, perhaps by some ghoulish tomb-raider cleaving its head from its shoulders, thus breaking the inner spell that bound her spirit to it. Their sins had surely found them out.

Rangda assumed her guise of merciless terror, ragged silver hair, large bulging eyes enflamed in cruelty and rage, long white fangs twitching for blood, her lolling tongue as of fire and blood, finger nails extended as if to flay human skin. "Fellow Councillors, yours it is to elect our king or queen. Shirina indeed has failed in honour, but did she not see rightly that Nindara had to go? Is there no praise of her boldness? And is it not clear that her cunning was undone by Alvah, not by herself? Is there no praise of her cunning? And was she not right to seek strength to reign? Is there no praise of strength? Only by her recourse to tradition would I fault her, save her betrayal of her liege lord and father, her denial of allegiance, and her lack of homage. Yet now a fresh chapter can begin. Our people can combine boldness, strength, and cunning, in one monarch, in one queen. I Rangda will be your queen, if you will." She stood forth.

The Great Council remained silent. Her words were wise, but was she their only choice, other than a no deal? Minutes passed. "Why your hesitancy, fellow Councillors?" asked Draven rising from his seat. "Is it not that you await another voice? I speak for the vampires, for I know their hearts. Let Kiskilla be our queen. As for cunning and strength, Rangda is rightly revered, but is not Kiskilla more so? Moreover, Kiskilla's bitter pain has fashioned her spirit, and she now is more reflective than reactive. A steadier hand to lead us, perhaps? I speak not against Rangda but for Kiskilla, but let Kiskilla herself speak."

"Fellow Councillors," said Kiskilla, arising from her seat, "I have hesitated to speak, but now must. I say clear that in days long gone I envied he who has gone, but would never have raised my hand against his throne, nay not even to seize it. But long now have I neither sought it nor envied him, for I have seen that the throne is but a shackle and its sovereign the shackled, though shackled to the subjects' freedom. As you at least know, my only child I butchered in jealousy—after she had family of her own and presumed to esteem them above me. And since being widowed I have had no men. I live in repentance and grieve day after day, seeking peace but finding none. At the death of our king I would have welcomed his family to reign, until I discovered their dishonour. Then the thought resurfaced that so long I had buried—that I might be queen—yet the thought was of fear. Hear ye, I seek it not, unless perhaps as penance for my sin. I seek it not, yet if ye seek me for it I shall not craven be. Unless then there be another, let now the Great Council choose between Kiskilla and bold Rangda." She too stood to stand before the council.

Long ages ago they had selected Nindara from five candidates. This time there was no selecting between an A and a B, then between that choice and a C, and so on and so forth. This time the cut would simply be between Kiskilla (who stood on their right) and Rangda (who stood on their left). Each councillor would close their eyes, then with a stone knife of pain in hand, cut their left or right arm, thus casting their vote. Then their votes would be seen by all—slashes to the left, slashes to the right. Politics wasn't for the squeamish, especially if there were many candidates to be voted on.

But this time no more needed to be said; both candidates were well known through long ages. One might be too rash; one might be too remorseful. But as the councillors extended their right arms, all were seen to bleed. As they extended their left arms, none were seen to bleed. What more needed to be said, save "Hail Kiskilla, queen of the vampires. Long live the queen!"

Three   Dreamworld

Lilith stirred. The sun was setting. The millennia had simply rolled by since her enthronement and her old names, and her kingdom was strong, stable, and secretive. With all the hallmarks of success, she was envied by her subjects. But long her imprisoned spirit had lain fast-bound in sin and nature's night. Her melancholy tears had long dried like the rings of Saturn, like the power of death, but still she felt them. Whyever had she murdered her own sweet Lona?

Her own husband, Tauresgal, a prince of the firstborn, had been killed in battle with the nephilim, when he had fought—against her better judgement—to save sons of Adam, a fragile few of the secondborn that had already been almost wiped from the face of the earth by mighty Toba's anger. Alas perhaps, that that seed had replenished itself, even though vampires could reap its harvest of blood. Alas beyond doubt, for the bitterness of her own loss had been such that she had vowed never to marry again: to love is to be vulnerable, and a lightless and loveless tomb is safer.

The nephilim had been an unauthorised experiment gone wrong, worse even than engineering a deadly virus, when in opposition to Nindara a mighty lord had arisen, and many vampires had followed him, mating with captured women of the firstborn. And then some of their sons had in turn mated with daughters of the secondborn! Daughters had not turned out so badly, though the sons had turned out somewhat larger sized than little monsters—giant monsters!

Nindara had finally ordered a purge of all surviving offspring. But that had neither been before the Nephilim War had wreaked havoc, nor before Usen himself had raised a gigantic flood—perhaps partly as a warning against future experiments—that had flooded the human psyche. Many myths had arisen to explain it; mighty Gilgamesh had dreamed of it and had had his turbulent dreamworld carved in stone.

For that day Usen's wrath had been great, for the hideous monsters had allied with many of the secondborn who were as sinful as themselves, and together had attacked the faithful of man who remained loyal to Usen. Few of their enemies had survived that war, and most of those who did so only survived as slaves subjugated by the mighty tide of the Black Force.

Offering no help, the firstborn's king Ránpalan had long stolen away to high ground, obeying a prophecy that forbade him from any alliance with man until the Yellow Dragon awoke the Fire of Surtur: the sindeldi king remained a hidden menace to Lilith's people. As the Black Force had swept over all the Light as a wave of Darkness, Necuratu, that faithless father of dunamoi, had smiled in silence.

But smiles can be short-lived. Few of the giants had survived after Usen had spoken; none seemingly after Nindara had spoken, though thereafter human gigantea were sometimes nicknamed nephilim, ghostly reminders of the unforgotten offspring of the Dark vampires and the firstborn. True, a rumour survived that one alone had survived both purges, one named Anaq, who in appearance was most like a man save for his added size—but what are rumours? Lilith's own daughter hadn't been a part of that experiment, and the secret daughter of her secret marriage had lived on in secret, married in secret, and mothered in secret. It was then that Lilith's jealousy kicked in and her secret crept out, at least to the Great Council. Alas, Lona's spilt blood had long dried into everlasting tears flowing within, but what was done was done.

Lilith's empathetic friend Ishtar had been one of the few to know and to comfort—sympathetic Draven had been another. That was partly why Lilith had adopted them. Few beyond the Great Council could be trusted to know of her disgrace. Even they only thought that it was her marriage, not her murder, which was her deep-felt disgrace, for most likened marriage to interspecies bestiality. No, she had repented of the murder but not the marriage.

Diplomatically a false story had been circulated, explaining away her true grief lest her love for one of—and offspring of—the firstborn, should imperil her life. Yet the dreamworld, disturbed by Lilith's lament, had produced various accounts of that murder; psychic resonances rippled through—and interweaved in—various patterns, patterns which many a human sleeper dreamed in tangled confusion: they who recorded their dreams for posterity at best hinted at the truth. Some dream stories even began to confuse her adopted son Draven with a Raven, or with Adam, or with both!

Lilith's dreamworld was troubled. She stirred, and her daughter-friend awoke. "Lilith, my queen, I grieve in your grief. Yet again I see that your daydreams have been evil. My mother, your heart you have locked up safe in the coffin of your selfishness, but do you not see, have I not said, that in that safe, dark, motionless coffin, it will change? Do you not see that though your heart will not be broken it will become unbreakable, impenetrable, and irredeemable? Likewise have I been entombed by myself, and speak from all too bitter experience." As if she had said too much or too little, she dropped her head in disquieted silence.

"Ishtar, my daughter-friend, I see now that you and I have both been in the valley of grief, yet I am doomed to remain longer within it. I know you speak the truth, but how can the truth set me free?" enquired Lilith doubtfully. "Peoples have known me by various names over time, and as Lilith, not Kiskilla, I am now known, but my heart, who can change?"

In the early days of their secondment within the Kingdom of Anu, there had been a certain amount of bitchiness. Yet they had even quarrelled over a mere huluppu tree, and some who mistold the story had believed her to be diabolic! They had long established mutual trust and reliance. Ishtar continued as adopted daughter of the queen, even as Draven had become her son, her *huiothesian*. Both should be capable of leading her people, but both had a publicly concealed gentleness and cared for her. Ishtar in particular puzzled Lilith. Was it that she had lost her bite?

Ishtar too had had her name changed by the secondborn, she who had been Inanna in Sumer which was no more, which long had been covered by the sands of time. Many names had she had in the long effaced past, long lost from human knowledge before the mountain of Sumer was even a mound in the ground. Worshipped by some as a goddess, like Lilith's her place among the divinities had been remarkable for a Dark vampire. For the Kingdom Power which watched over Mesopotamia had allowed an interface with the Dark vampires—perhaps in hope of their redemption.

The divinities could blunder and cause chaos in crotchety anger, yet for the main part were kind and benevolent towards Usen's children. Guardians were they against the diaboloi. Their hope unhidden was that if the vampires were redeemed from the Dark Side, then they—

the divinities—would have a strong ally in their struggles with the diaboloi. The Dark vampires were not natural enemies of either side, though much more at home with the Necros, for they were of the Night. Even so, it was useful to have someone with a foot in the divinities' camp. Thus Nindara had been happy to send Inanna—later known as Ishtar—into Anu's kingdom, Mesopotamia's imperfect yet rough bulwark against the Turannoi.

Her stint with the Powers had ended by promotion to princess. A good student, Ishtar had learned much of their mind, which was as they too had wished—yet they had also wished that she would have learnt much of their heart. It might have been different had she dwelt a while in Necuratu's kingdom! However, all that was past. For long now she had dwelt in a place called, by Siwel the Jester, Niatirb, yet Angleland by the serious Saxons, who jested seldom save in the safety of their few remaining halls. Once it had been a good place for white slaves, slaves so fair of face that some had mistook *angli* for *angeli*, but they were never angels. The vampire kingdom had relocated its hidden palace there long before the local culture war had begun. Now the Angevins there held a whip in their right hand, with their left squeezing the Saxon lords into their own mould—diversification was bad. So what? Vampires didn't mind which farmer looked after the herd.

That night Ishtar and her mother arose to a full moon. A fine mist shrouded the forest. Together they flew from their cave, taking in the wonderful woods of Shirewude, with its vast and mighty oaks—the dryads and hamadryads had long departed in ancient days to the Island of Woods. Unlike the diaboloi, vampires were lovers of nature, and even Earth—a speck of dust in the cosmos—filled them full with wonder. No wonder, for it was designed as a taster for Usen's children in their infancy. Even the sindeldi had a saying that it was never wooden to see a new tree.

Gliding above the tree tops they sailed over an ocean of wonder. Most of their flight was sightseeing, both at the woods below and deep heaven above. In fact most of their lives were spent in a sleep state, slowing their rate of degradation, and dwelling on the past, or in the nights enjoying the night life of heaven and earth. For the strongest of them, food wasn't daily or even weekly, for even a little blood converted into their sinews, went a long way. Some hunted every full moon; some once a year; some once a century. They might drink for pleasure, not need. Each had their own pattern. It was only the more playful among them who played cat and mouse with humans—or the occasional sindeldi or hob caught alone at night, but the Cave Kingdom, adopted by Usen, never let its guard down, and wasn't much fun to play with anyway. Some pitied those of Usen's children whom they would cut short from Earth's pleasures, but most vampires found such pity puzzling. Did humans pity the sheep they slew for stew?

After a while, Ishtar and Lilith went their different ways. Long they had flown together, and neither needed to say or to ask when they should fly alone—they were not tied to the hip. When it felt right for her, Lilith simply glided away from Ishtar. Always they ate alone. Lilith had hunted some days earlier. She had found a hamlet where a young baby lay at the point of death. The parents were hard working peasants with limited means for medicines, medicines which mainly took the form of herbs. Knowing which herbs were right, and getting them even if you knew, was the trick. The baby was beyond the pale, and Lilith intended to return to quietly put it out of its misery.

A recent cosmic event, little over a millennium ago now, had taught her that Usen's children never exactly died—that adjusted her aioniology. Not that their fate mattered to her, since she had never pitied her infant victims. Why should she, when they never had more than days before death anyway? In fact she kind of envied them. For the death of the body was not the death of the soul, and she now saw that at death the destiny of the Psuchai was to fly off to judgement. Those with a heart for Usen would be welcomed by him; others were welcome to depart into the emptiness never created for them, a bleak emptiness where she herself would undoubtedly meet some of her victims in Necuratu's kingdom—would they eternally haunt her? But for now they helped stave off death. She had neither hatred nor love towards the human race, being content to take only that which soon—even in their short innings—would die. Yet in the weeping of mothers she too as a mother bereft, wept.

Each went their different ways. Lilith had flown away for her meal. Ishtar rose higher and circled, ensuring that her queen-mother showed no interest in her whereabouts. Political correctness required all to be dedicated to the proposition that human blood should be their primary food, and that vampires should show their food neither hope nor hatred. Though self-evident, the fact remained that some had soft consciences, hiding it even from their friends. One never knew if a friend might turn into a fiend, betraying vital confidences. So if you didn't agree with the script, it was best to fake it. They had no police, secret or otherwise, yet they had local courts that would examine charges laid against villainous vampires.

Ishtar always needed to look over her shoulders when she went out to dine. This night was no different. Having parted with Lilith she flew southwards some hundred or so miles, into Brademore Wood of the River Aleburne. There lived a hamlet of Ulvritone, the manor of Ernulf de Hesdin. It had a dozen or so households of villagers and smallholders, and its future seemed secured by the noble knight. Ernulf himself had left on the crusade aimed at freeing lands from Muslim expansionism, else his help might have been sought. For therein lay an ill man, the common cure—leeching—providing excellent cover for any vampire pretending to drink only human blood.

It was not to the ill man that she went, but into the wooded canopy she glided, then changed her course, soon landing on a branch and checking that no snoopy bats lurked around about. What she had planned was dangerous. What she had planned was catching rabbits. This was easy in execution, for which her thanks went to the Normans who had reintroduced rabbits into the country, rabbits which she had soon released from their coneygarths. By now she had acquired a taste for them. She knew from experience that human blood was richer, however for long she had followed the religion of peace, seeing herself—and humans—in Usen's likeness, not in Necuratu's image.

Her *modus operandi* was now to reconnoitre nights before feeding, choosing warrens that lay near to some hamlet or other where she knew some patient was being leeched, a process that in the hands of amateur practitioners like barbers—or even the more skilled hands of monks and priests—could lead to death, and which Ishtar could pretend to be her orthodox handiwork. Orthodoxy said that human life was secular, but that animal life was sacrosanct.

What of her real victims? They slept blissfully unaware, dreaming perhaps of their Guardian Power, Frith (a picture in their dream-pool matrix given by Usen). To them came not the Black Rabbit of whom they dreamed (in their dreams the terminator yet agent of Light), but one cloaked as a tiny little bat, one silently stalking like a thief in the night. They who would feel neither pain nor fear, and would soon feel nothing at all as sleep seamlessly shifted into oblivion.

The Great Teacher had taught his secondary students to picture coneys as representing the unkosher, the abnorm, along with all animals that didn't represent the symbolic norm of both partial separation from the accursed ground of death, and of spiritual rumination of life. It was a unique status which only his students could achieve, and a complex symbolism that had helped prepare the way for the college class of Hamashiach, who had done away with the literalism of the preparatory symbolism, even as a chick foregoes its shell. Likewise ingesting other's blood had for illustration purposes been a class taboo, never a wrong in itself. *"Surge Petre, occide et manduca"* she said silently to herself with a smile. She and her mother had gone their different ways. It was safe to eat.

Four   GRINDAN'S FATE

Back in the year of our lord 1066, Land-Ravager had fallen at Stamford Bridge, and the Norwegians had surrendered to Harold the Saxon king, who in turn had fallen before the Norman Norsemen—he who had been befriended by Torquil Wolfganger the Builder, had given seven feet and gained six. The Conqueror, once cousin to the Confessor—for family trees are pruned by death—had come, he whom some called a bastard. Normanisation, foreshadowed by Edward, made unsteady progress. Tostig Godwinson, erstwhile earl on the grave of Sigeweard, and slayer of Ulf son of Dolfin, had fallen and his body had visited France—but he had had his revenge. Gundulf the Monk, whose hand would build the White Tower, had sent a cryptic warning to Walleff, Earl of Huntingdon: "Let your people beware this year, lest the bat overshadow the daughter of the bold and the bear."

1066! The years had flown by since those lazy, hazy, crazy days of Sumer, and all seemed well, but trouble was stirring like a witches' brew. Within Lilith's kingdom lived many vampires, most in family camps, many blending in with the humans. The vampires were past masters of deception, among themselves and to outsiders. One such camp was led by Marwolaeth. As daylight approached, she returned as usual to their lair. As usual her daughter Kendra and her son Wulfgar had returned before her to the pleasant cool of the dark, but her second son, Grindan Sceadugenga, was still awaited.

Of course her children were all equals by adoption, a convenient way for a small camp to live within—or within the outskirts of—human society. Fitting in was their forté. Before the coming of Usen's children it hadn't been so, and they still felt sore that they needed to fit in with wings clipped. And though they predated humanity, with whom they generally got along quite nicely, many of their kind were now feeling the pinch of the ages. Vampires were not as vigorous as they used to be, for time was taking its toll.

Earth itself was not as it had been before man was introduced, man the hunter-gatherer. Man had made substantial changes in domesticating the land, but much remained wild. Marwolaeth's family, as with her people generally, enjoyed human company. One could say that in fact they had an acquired taste for it. And human society was generally happy with them, but it was the happiness of ignorance. There were many humans who lived on the fringe of many societies, people of the woods, the rivers, or the shores. There were hermits who sought isolation; the crazed of mind; outlaw bands under pretence of petty merchantmen; wandering tinkers unsafe to meet where the wood was dark and the grass was green; knights of the black market. The family of Marwolaeth were far different from human peripatetics. The family of Marwolaeth had once wandered the Milky Way in search of a new home.

Grindan had set off immediately after dusk to see Sybil Fitz-Siward, for reasons of a personal nature. Why confide when you can conceal? He certainly hadn't told his mother. At the end of the day she wasn't a day older then he, even if she was leader of the camp, and to ask advice was a sign of weakness. The lady's brother was Walleff the Saxon, not a man to be trifled with, and not some powerless human, either, but the Earl of Huntington with the strength to back that up. Sybil was in fact a sweet girl, and her position was a good one to infiltrate, for combined with her looks she was likely to marry into a very noble family. "Faint heart never won fair lady", he had chuckled to Kendra, as soon as mother had left for a late night snack. And she had smiled as one sharing a joke. She was not smiling now. Had her brother gone too far? Mother had returned as dawn dawned.

"I'm concerned", said mother. "I know you couldn't have stopped him—he has always been too full of himself—but you should've come after me. We could at least have followed to keep watch over him. For our numbers only decrease, we who should be masters of the world."

"He will be back soon, don't worry. It has been so long since he's enslaved a woman, he's been tensing up for almost a century now. You know that we have got to give him his head now and again, mother", replied Kendra boldly. If she felt concern, she was hiding it well. In fact she was hiding it well. Grindan was very much a night creature of regular habits. Although his mission was irregular—to bond rather than to bleed—he could easily have been back by now, and should have been. Of their camp he was the most sensitive to light. All were finding light more painful than even a millennium ago, but he had gotten to a point where even a bright moon was something he found hard to bear.

His night had begun well. Ever since moving into the area, Sybil had been stalked, though it had begun innocently enough. One night he had been having a wee bit of fun with a woodsman, whom he had smelt out when feeling a wee bit peckish. On that night sheer devilment had been upon him, and when in such playful mood he would often play cat to mouse. The woodsman had had no chance, alone in the forest. But it was full early, and Grindan had been a bit bored. No quick kill for him, but in human form he accosted the woodsman—to him merely a nameless victim. The woodsman tasted fear; Grindan tasted blood. Just a snick at first, then he allowed the terrified man to run.

After a few more minutes he pounced from the side, using his fingers like claws to rip, rather than his teeth to drink. A little more blood, a little more terror, a little more run run running in vain. It was pleasant to see such futile flight, and then another snick, and then another. Eventually he tired of the game, and dispatched his quarry. He had had his fill, then as a bat he flew around the neighbourhood castle sitting high on its motte, soon spotting the new girl in the neighbourhood high up in her keep.

As always the guards patrolled in twos, as they had done ever since an unexplained death of a solitary lookout on its walls, whose corpse in daylight lacked colour, lacked blood. There were enough local stories to warrant superstition, and after that the guards had insisted on always having backup. Little did they know that killing two would have only taken twice as long. Let's see, that would have been about two seconds.

But Grindan's camp was not permitted to draw too much attention to dark tales. There existed both professional and amateur vampire slayers, few and far between maybe, but best kept in the dark even though they had little power to slay. The real danger was in humans ganging up and cornering them, not superstitious individuals sporting silver bow, arrow, or cross. Those of their own kind who opposed them, were far more deadly. For vampires of the Dawn—who unnaturally revelled in the sunshine—were in the night as deadly as owls to bats. Keeping nuisance levels down normally kept them at bay. But Grindan was arrogant, not afraid to throw caution to the wind. Guards added to the game. When he spotted the earl's daughter attired for bed but reading by her window in the candlelight, he quietly alighted and watched, perched head down directly above her window.

When the vampires had first taken humanoid DNA, they had modelled themselves on the firstborn. The bat form was simply a convenient mode for flight, easy enough for a shapeshifter, but not DNA based. Vampires never really fancied real bats, but humans, well, they were tasty flesh and blood, weren't they, fair game? Sybil had caught his eye—both evil eyes in fact. Her social standing protected her from a mere seduction or slaying—though the former could double as the latter. Idly at first the feeling had grown that it was high time to add a slave to his camp. What mother would think, he neither knew nor cared. Act first, then face the consequences, was his motto. That first night had ended with the beginnings of a plot, and returning to their lair he had even forgotten to recount the comedy of the unhappy woodsman. The stalking of Sybil had begun in earnest.

Ironically the stalking of Grindan had begun, unbeknown to himself. For nights ago the guards had noticed a solitary bat hanging around, and superstition had stirred their recent fears. Lord Walleff now sat down to breakfast, looking as a teenage man does who has been awoken at the break of dawn, then has had others awoken to brainstorm vitally urgent matters. This morning their breakfast was laid, then their servants left the hall—except for one who remained seated in a dark corner. "Sister, please don't be alarmed, but early this morning I was told that my guards fear that you are being watched at nights", said Walleff pacifically. Ironically she had only recently been moved to this castle in response to a mysterious monk's warning! Her brother was staying with some force of arms while she settled in.

Sybil laughed merrily: "Why brother, that is ridiculous. My boudoir is at the top of the keep, where I can look down on all but none can look down on me. My room can't even be seen from the castle wall. Oh brother, you're always making such a fuss about nothing, one week it's this, another it's that. Come now, my door is strong and none but I get through it at nights. Mayhap the guards have been unguarded in their cups?" She smiled sweetly, unafraid of the world while with her little brother.

"I wish it were as simple as that" he said. "No, days ago the guards informed their captain, who placed extra guards under cover, watching your chambers. It is as he was told. A vagrant bat has become a regular visitor. The chief guard didn't want to speak until he was sure, but if anything untoward had happened to you while he dallied, he would surely have danced at the end of a rope. Nay, do not laugh, for I have heard strange stories from the lore master about a bat race known by some as vampyrs. It is said that they can possess the minds and wills of those they enslave, and can walk as men, fly as bats, or run like wolves. No, Sybil, I have just cause for concern, and so have you." He kept dark his real fears for her safety, and why he and his lore master and master builder had accompanied them to this castle. She wasn't thick, and had suspected some rumour of kidnap or vendetta, but this was totally *outré*.

"But, if your fears are justified, how can I be safe? Must my only window be blocked up? Can't our bowmen shoot this bat from hell into hell, and be done with it?" It really was a bit much to turn her into a prisoner in her own home. You can take protection too far, you know.

"I'm afraid it's not so easy, if ancient lore be true. But we have come up with a plan. Firstly you will be moved to a more reclusive room, with guards outside and always maids in your chamber to keep watch at night. It is said that vampires only stalk at night. Next, in your own room Nerienda your maid shall dress like you at nights, keeping her face from the window, and another shall act as her maid. The master builder says that he can construct a metal cage around your bed, concealed by its curtains, allowing a bat to fly in through a hidden trapdoor that can be dropped and bolted at will. Guards can be placed so as to see without being seen: if this creature flies in it will be caught, a bat in a trap."

"But dear Walleff, won't my maids be in danger, and how can a cage contain a bat anyway? Isn't it all much ado about nothing?" Her brother didn't reply but called forth his master builder from the shade, who in turn unravelled some parchments, laying out the design he had begun sketching out. Sybil's wooden bed—beautiful but not quite the famed four post elven bed of Dá Chích Anann—would be moved so that the headpiece would back onto her window. Given the warm balmy nights, this would make sense to any snoop.

In daylight hours the drapes would be lowered, while smithies wrought the panelled cage. In nighttime hours any nocturnal visitor would see only the suspended canopy, and the curtains—suspended from the ceiling—draped around the sides, while the end section of cage would be raised out of sight. The visitor would see the wakeful maid and the seemingly slumbering lady, and probably bide its time. Yet lest it should unguardedly enter, guards should be hidden behind the curtains. Only once the smiths had finished building their metal cage—even the bed would be positioned over metal panelwork— would the maid feign sleep. Further back in the chamber, as befitted her, she would be safe, while the bed would be made up to make it seem that Sybil slept ensconced within.

"Then shall we see what we shall see", concluded Walleff. Sybil seemed satisfied, although her brother had not fully answered her questions. She knew that he was anxious, and could say more than he had. Yes, it did seem over the top simply because a little bat had hung around her window a few nights, yet she trusted him implicitly, knowing that he cared lovingly for her, and that he was not easily alarmed. And so she held her peace. As brother and sister they had bonded well through the sorrows of life. Their mother Ælfflæd, granddaughter on her maternal side to Uhtred, had died sorrowfully in her first year; their older half-brother Bulux the Axe had fallen bravely by the hand of MacBeth in the Battle of the Seven Sleepers in her sixth year; and their father, Sigeweard Bearsson, had died as a cow—not as an ox— in her seventh. Her brother, befriended by Edward the Confessor, had turned out to be a charitable Christian, though less charitable to Normans.

The nights past with Sybil sleeping on a much inferior bed, though carpenters had, for reason unknown to her, begun to craft a new bed. She missed her mattress and encurtained privacy, but curiously her brother had assured her that by Christ's Mass her troubles should, God willing, be over. For her that fatal night began badly, with her tossing and turning in her unfamiliar bed. In contrast, for Grindan that night had begun well. Leaving Kendra, he had flown low over the scarp and noticed that the garrison guards were less thick on the ground. Then peering in through Sybil's window, he saw with satisfaction that the maid's insomnia had been cured, for there she lay at the other side of the room, snoring loud enough to wake the dead.

Yet the lady slept on, only the outline of her body betrayed by the quilt. So long as he slew none, nor was spotted by any, his infiltration was simple. Fluttering in to this sleeping beauty he would gently bite her neck, injecting the DNA of his will to modify hers and subdue her to his will. None but she would know that thereafter wherever she went, he went, that whatever she saw and heard, he could see and hear. She would inevitably marry among the rich and famous, giving him access to useful inside information. At last, in he gently fluttered, next to the covered head.

Did this daughter of Eve not know that it wasn't safe for her kind to inhale their exhaled air! He facetiously wondered how many of her little grey cells would be damaged by her folly. But his inner laughter was immediately cut-short, for guards hidden within who had watched like hawks, had cut the cord, releasing the end panels.

The trap was sprung. He heard the sound of bolting and double bolting on the outside. After that, silence. The almost pitch black cage agitated Grindan. The head resting next to him was a straw dummy, and he felt a dummy himself to be caught off guard by vermin. He had underestimated these humans.

He tore the tapestry down, finding only metal above. The cage was inescapable for him, since of the ice clan he could no longer vaporise and rebuild his solid body, nor liquefy and reharden. Nor could he shape-shift small enough to get through the tiny vents along the base, or the holes above. His chance might come when eventually they raised one of the dropped panels to view their prisoner. Humans were creatures of curiosity. He could quietly bide his time. He could lie a hundred years on ice and not freeze. And though he could not drink a river of blood and not burst, he could fast for a thousand years and not die. He could easily outlast these creatures. Yet it wouldn't come to that. Kendra would soon tell their mother all she knew. Mother would rescue him before many nights were out. She would punish him, no doubt, but surely she would not betray him to the local courts as one who had endangered their hiddenness? He shivered at the very thought. He must just—but hello, what was happening. Some smelly liquid was dribbling through the holes above.

Shock reality struck home. They meant to kill, not cage him. The metal could contain a furnace. The fools would burn down their house to burn down his! No, they would have readied water to drench their wooden keep. Only he would burn. Taking human form he cried out for mercy, promising all kinds of things he had no intention of giving. "Mercy, mercy", from he who showed no mercy.

But from those to whom no mercy would be shown, no mercy was given. Flickering tongues of fire appeared at the lowest parts of the sides. Only now did he realise the significance of the straw covered floor. A quick look under the bed revealed flammable stuffing. Suffocating smoke was beginning to rise as a wreath. In blind panic he went berserk. "The skies shall fall, the earth shall gape, blood and fire will obliterate your world! Release me, mercy! You will be accursed! Spare me!"

His only reply was the inexorable drip drip drip of yet more oil. A vampire can only take so much heat before its spirit can no longer keep its body together. It was not a question of pain but of physics. Of the ice-clan, his body and spirit could part in death, yet reunite after millennia and be refreshed. But that was under normal conditions. Intense incineration was a totally abnormal condition. Throwing away all hope he threw away his body and departed to the final judgement, never again to trouble the earth. It would soon forget him, but his mother would remember the offence and the blood feud now begun with the House of Huntingdon, and a greater bitterness towards the human vermin in general.

Five   Blood Feud

Marwolaeth vowed revenge. It was not that she had loved her son—she would have spurned the very thought. Vampires bonded for strength and security, not for affection. True, companionship could comfort the soul, and there were rumours of rebel vampires who had bonded with Usen's children for love. Personally she believed that those rumours were pernicious accusations against fellow vampires, to destroy or demean those one hated. Hate was a well respected emotion. No, no one grieved Grindan's death, but it deeply affected Marwolaeth's pride. It was not fitting for humans to dare to raise their hands against one of her noble kind. They must pay.

Still, she used her anger to cover up the fact that he hadn't confided in her his intent—she who had been his very mother! The ingrate hadn't respected her, and she'd feel better by lashing out. To vampires, a thousand years was as a day, and it would have been nice to let the prey stew in its own juice for millennia, but this prey was short lived on Earth. So after only a few years Marwolaeth opened up her mind. "My children, I have a plan to revenge ourselves on the line of Walleff. Will you help me or hinder me?"

That was sooner than expected, but expected. "Mother, we too seek revenge. A family that neither averts nor avenges the death of its own, is held in contempt by our people. Revenge is expected of us, in spite of the queen. What then is your plan?" enquired Kendra.

"Walleff has now regained his earldom and is married, and that for what they call love. Soon they will wed and bed. It is from this great height that we will sink him down into the slough of despond. Wife and children he shall have, yet he shall see both under our curse, for he shall not pay the penalty for his sin alone. We will snatch from his arms his beloved wife, and send into exile his first-born. His earldom shall be divided and brought to an end—*mene, mene, parsin*. He shall be betrayed and beheaded. Our queen need not know of our curse, but he shall know it and in that knowledge despair and die. For we will shadow his comings and goings, and be a snare to him and his, and he shall know that revenge is ours and we will repay", hissed Marwolaeth.

∞

After an early disobedience, Walleff had returned to the good books of King William and had met a lovely young damsel of Norman stock, sweet Constance of York. Soon it was when their vows were witnessed and they might lawfully live together as husband and wife. Their wedding was of dual religions, for Walleff was cautious about abandoning the divinities of his ancestors. Thus it was that an old Saxon weofodthegn had invoked the blessings of Wodan and of Frigg. Walleff had then surrendered Siward's sword into his in-laws' safekeeping, to be handed back to his firstborn son and heir.

The hunigmonap, the honeymoon, had begun, but the next day a second wedding took place, just to be on the safe side, officiated by a priest of the crux religion. The handgeld had been paid, but only on the second morning was the morning gift handed over to the bride. Dual ceremonies done, the happy couple could begin to settle into full married bliss. That that was sweet was obvious to all who met them, and in the fullness of time a child of their love was born into this world, Egbert, and a great banquet was held in his honour.

Among the guests there came a fell woman of mystery—blood red fire leaked out from her staff. "Hail, Earl of Huntingdon, mighty warrior of the axe. Hear now my words of knowledge, for I see into the future, even as the wondrous Sybil did see. Alas, vengeance is set for you to swallow as a bitter herb. For Thurbrand the Hold killed Uhtred the Bold your mother's grandfather. In his turn The Hold was slain by her father Ealdred, who in turn was slain by Carl son of The Hold. It is thus for you to slay in turn the sons and grandson of Carl, whether you will or nill, thou who art double minded.

"Weep o man, for vengeance is set upon you and your house, vengeance inescapable. For you wantonly slew a creature nobler and more ancient than thine own house. Fool, did you not know that it had those who would avenge its death? For your sin and folly, unto you is allotted the disinheritance of your firstborn, and your heir shall divide your spoils, until your inheritance be forgot. Your wife shall be lost to you, and shall betray you, until your head parts from the body. Feast now and rejoice now with despair, for with the rising sun sorrow will walk with you. But I am merely a prophet of your loss." The seer turned on her heels and stalked away through the hushed guests. None dared stay her.

Thus it was that Kendra delivered her words of doom, striking terror into the heart of Walleff. Despair would one day give way to hope, but for now he stood gobsmacked, bereft of voice. His ancestors of the far north knew of such seers, and also those of the new religion. The power of seers was undoubted, yet it was said that they could be cheated. What if he killed his wife? How could she then betray him? Yet priests spoke of a slain whose blood cried out for justice. Perhaps killing her would cause her to betray him after death? But no, whatever might come, he was sure of her love for him and his love for her. Besides, he had committed himself to her for life, and whether he loved or loathed her was incidental to that vow, his pledged word.

That's what covenant meant. If she would be his death, so be it; he should not be hers. Herein the new religion spoke clear: turn the other cheek; bless those who persecute you falsely. But it was his own heart and will that dictated his thoughts. He looked to Constance, giving her a reassuring smile. She had stood silent, afraid that she would come to betray him, wondering if that meant that he would first betray her with another woman. Why else would her newborn son be disinherited? What had her beloved done that a blood feud had begun? After the guests had left, Walleff shared with his spouse the story of how his sister had been stalked, and how a prophecy from Gundulf had warned him to beware of a bat. In the sharing of his woes the couple became even closer than ever, and would stoically await their fates. As it was, fate intervened all too soon with the death of Constance, leaving Walleff to be a single father. She had not betrayed him.

Thus it was that William the king proposed that Walleff should take his noble niece, the Lady Judith of Lens, to wife. Should not Egbert, son of Walleff, have a mother? Should not Walleff, father of Egbert, have a wife? And in this marriage the lands of the earl would be tied the stronger to the throne, and so too the realm of the Saxons to their Norman overlord. So it was that after a time of grieving Walleff united with Judith, and Marwolaeth smiled. For she had planned to tempt Constance into betrayal, but Constance had unexpectedly died. And Constance had been, well, constant, and betrayal had not been part of her nature.

Marwolaeth could not foresee the future, merely plan it, but could adjust her plan of attack. Judith was a different kettle of fish than Constance had been. Judith was for Judith, more apt to betrayal, especially if feeling slighted. And thus it was that she fitted well with Marwolaeth. For egged on by her, Walleff arranged the assassination of the offspring of Carl. And yet its success did not sit well with him. Soon after, he played the fool in joining friends in a revolt against the king. With the spilling of yet more blood his heart revolted, and in heaviness of heart he turned to Archbishop Lanfranc for wisdom and forgiveness.

"My lord Archbishop, I have by foul hand committed bloody deeds in blood feud, and joined in unrighteous conspiracy against my rightful liege lord. My soul is in turmoil; my life is in jeopardy. My lord, please grant unto me the peace of the church" begged Walleff on bended knee.

"My child, you are divided and confused. As you have rightly said, on the House of Carl you have sinned greatly. Do you not see that returning hate for hate multiplies hate, adding deeper darkness to a night already bereft of stars? Darkness cannot drive out Darkness; only Light can do that. Hate cannot drive out hate; only love can do that. Your allegiance to friends and lord is divided, as is your allegiance to the old and the new religions. You doubt whether the new is better than the old, and so are divided. If your little ones ask you who created the world, or what awaits them after the tomb, will you answer that you have no idea?

"You do not doubt that good is real, yet know that like you Wodan is not fully good. Do you not see that both can only be judged by a standard if the standard, the fully good, exists? Is the true standard not Goodness, God himself by very nature? If there is no standard there is no ought at all, no ought to do good at all, no right to side with or to oppose, and life would be meaningless.

"I do not doubt the power of Wodan, but he serves imperfectly under an ultimate power, the power over all powers. The error of the old ways was not seeing that king as being an emissary, not the end. That error is dimness, short-sight. Will you not turn to the Light? Have you not been told of prophecies of an anointed one who would die and rise again to begin a new kind of people? Have you not been told that he was our champion, battling by his death with Diabolos, and defeating death for us? Why not turn fully to his way of love and peace? Why have one foot in both camps—a hedging of bets?" Lanfranc with many words sought to persuade Walleff concerning messiah, from morning until evening. Much they reasoned together, until Walleff finally bowed his head in penitence. The good had been a thief to the best, a limiter of truth. And he saw that being open to the truth afforded him a light to travel and a hope beyond the journey. His offences were forgiven; a kingdom beyond the world was his, and the king over all high kings.

"Now as regards your rebellion, do not wait for the king to return, but go rather to him in contrition. I shall send with you a letter of commendation, but he is a stern king, and I cannot foresee how things will go, my son."

"Gramercy good father, for now my heart and mind are at one and at rest. I shall go in hope and bow my knee—and if he wills my head also," said Walleff with a new smile of tranquillity.

And so it was that he sailed across the waters, not away from danger but towards it. Yet this was not the will of Marwolaeth, and she was wrath. In response to this unexpected conversion she sent Kendra, a stranger to Judith, to allege Walleff's infidelity as her paramour. Wulfgar went as her brother, demanding payments from Judith to cover up Walleff's misdemeanours, and to cover a paternity suit for which they claimed him guilty. Judith, now a mother of children, was livid with rage. How dare he cheapen her, especially with a wench of low birth? She didn't doubt it, for these accusers seemed genuine and staked their lives on the truth of their claims.

Judith had already been angered that her husband had sided with other earls against her uncle the king. He had ignored her over that, and so far she had kept quiet. Indeed she feared lest the king's anger encompass her, and hoped to weather the storm. If the earls won she might gain more land; if they lost she could claim ignorance of Walleff's connivance and keep his lands. But Walleff had again wavered, this time away from rebellion, and had headed off to the archbishop for absolution. Enough to try the patience of any wife! On top of all that he had dishonoured their marriage bed. Well, enough was enough. He had betrayed her. It was now time for her to betray him. Nor would Egbert be spared if she could help it—why should her children not succeed Walleff?

So it was that Walleff did not escape vampire vengeance. Walleff had sought out William in Normandy, and was returning under suspicion when news came of a Danish fleet in the Humber. William suspected that Walleff was a snake in the grass, an enemy in the guise of a friend. Then came word from Judith of insider knowledge of Walleff's duplicity and design upon the throne. That was the clincher.

Although Lanfranc had testified to Walleff's recanted disloyalty, Lanfranc no doubt had been deceived—why, Walleff's own wife had dobbed him in! Enough was enough. Walleff would die under the executioner's axe, and his estates and title would go to loyal Judith. The trial was a foregone conclusion. It would be a matter of public knowledge that, on May 31, in the year of our lord 1076, Walleff was beheaded, as painfully slowly he prayed the Paternoster at Saint Gile's Hill near Winchester. It would also be a matter of public rumour that the bodiless head would slowly finish the prayer, "deliver us from evil", and that body and head would rejoin after both were retrieved from ignominy by Abbot Ulfkettle. By order of the king, Egbert was cast off from inheritance and sent into exile with a pittance, left to the guardianship of two old faithful retainers. Revenge had come with a vengeance.

Even so, Marwolaeth wasn't fully satisfied. Over time the earldom passed in theory to Judith. Yet she, unhappy with a replacement husband proposed by King William, fled in defiance and to his displeasure. In time her eldest daughter Matilda, inheriting the title, married he who had been set to marry her mother, and the inheritance soon became debatably divided between her offspring to two husbands, and would soon be dispossessed. Marwolaeth would leave her calling cards along the way. Egbert had escaped with his life, but he too would be haunted, would be shadowed, would come under the curse of the vampires. He, rightful heir of Huntingdon, could live out his days in fear of his life and love again. And for a time Marwolaeth's anger rested in the pleasure of its firstfruit: her *shavuot* would be its setting.

The year was 1184, and in merry England the House of Plantagenet had recently been divided between the Young King and his father, Henry 2, always the senior king of the kingdom. The young Henry, never now to be the Third, had fought alongside his brother Richard, fallen out with brother and father, and had died. Many had favoured the Young King—a dashing young man with a flair for the martial arts—but to come out and commit to him had been a dangerous luxury best left to the powerful few who could afford it, and definitely not for young ladies. But young ladies could afford the royal house to bicker all it liked, supplying them with rumours and counter rumours of dark and deep intrigues, in short, tasty morsels of court gossip. They were too young and too protected to fear. That chapter had been sealed by death, but the house remained divided, and the gossiping continued.

The Lady Marian Fitz-Walter was due tomorrow. Perhaps that is why Ulrica dreamed what she dreamed, for that night she dreamed that her world was pitch black, yet soon awoke a glow on the horizon. Birds, only two or three at first, began their chorus, both a beauty and an affliction to the sleepless. She had quickly dressed for the merrymaking of the day, when a knock on the door announced her friend. "Marian, please do come in and welcome." The two young women smiled at each other, quickly admiring each other's dress. Blackbirds sang, and somewhere a robin. Together the ladies saddled up and rode out for Maying, a gorgeous day on which to gather blossoms to decorate the Maypole. Their squires too wore garlands of fresh leaves on their heads, and horns were at their sides. In the warmth they stopped in a glade besides a fountain which flowed forth from the earth, and dismounted.

In her dream it was May Day. May Day ushered in the season of courtship, gladdening the heart. Both ladies were at an age when marriage was on their minds—had been for years! Marian, 19 years to her 18. Marian, the happy-go-lucky—who sometimes disguised as a shepherdess—and a whizz at archery—as befits they who love sheep and hate wolves.

Today neither thought of wolves, neither the four nor the two-legged kind. Ulrica spoke gigglingly of her crush on young Wilfred, Cerdic's son, though she—and his father—was angry with him for going off on the crusade. Marian supported her choice: "Although Norman in name, my heart is to those oppressed by my people. That is why—you must never tell—I even go in disguise among them as Clorinda the Shepherdess, to dance carefree yet to learn of injustices that I can help amend. Let Norman pay for Norman misdeeds.

"Alas, little does my beloved father know that free access to his coffers means that I smuggle money to his Saxon serfs. His heart of gold would never understand me secretly spending his silver to help his subdued serfs, any more than me helping crippled sheep. The proud Norman mind seldom minds because it seldom sees, since it always looks down. Oh for Norman and Saxon to become Briton! After all, young Wilfred's heart is given to *le quor de lion*, showing that Saxon will gladly serve Norman if Norman be good. But much evil is still to come, or so I have been warned by my father confessor, the Prophet of Copmanhurst, whom some call the Mad Monk Michael."

In her dream Ulrica had chuckled that Michael was indeed a mad monk, whose reputation as a mystic was only exceeded by his reputation with wine, which was why the jolly *Frere* preferred his feasts over his fasts, and his tuck to his toast. True, though he shared that reputation with Brothers who seemed unscarred by the marks of self-denial, unlike them he seemed shy of stealing from the lay, even from lowly surfs, even from those of the blood of Jews and of infidels, and avoided other worldly pleasures even more inconsistent with monastic vows. Well, perhaps the best apple in the tub, but you had to admit that he was still the Batty Brother. "Alas dearest Marian, even I am prophet enough to see that evils will long plague our divided kingdom, for man is born for trouble as surely as sparks fly upward. What if anything does Brother Michael teach to our profit besides this?"

In her dream Marian had not replied, for the ghostly spectre of Michael had arisen from the fountain's pool. "Ulrica, beware, lest you bake bread for pharaoh. Beware lest soon you hear the prison doors close behind you, and crusts be your lot until your head be exalted in flames, when by your hand those who have brought you low shall at last be cast down below you. Death shall be the husband you will have long pined for, unless you forsake this very day your father for the father of him you seek, Torquilstone for Rotherwood. Marian, blessèd are you among women, yet you shall not be blessed by fruit of your womb. For seeking the true way you shall be imprisoned in maidenhood. Yet rejoice, for your deeds will long be praised. For you shall taste wine for pharaoh. After the travail of your soul you will rejoice, and he whom you will marry will in truth be him long awaited. Yet his bride must surrender to become what some will call another's bride, unless in fear you choose to flee your blessing. My children, beware your fates, and pray for strength to endure." Ulrica awoke. Boy, even in her dreams the Mad Monk gave her the creeps!

In the real world the day broke, and the two girls met at the May Day festival of Torquilstone Castle. The vividness of the dream was such that Ulrica repeated word for word the message of the spectre, "totally weird, but don't let that spoil our fun" she added to Marian. Marian pondered the words in her heart, but soon succumbed to the spirit of the celebrations. Many a peasant had been allowed into the courtyard to celebrate that day, for many the highest of days apart from Withus and Atonewith days. Even from Norfolk had come the heir of Turkil Hako, a well-known hawker and somewhat crooked, but a happy to meet man.

Less happily, within a small tent into which their daring and curiosity had led them, a gypsy woman had predicted a happy fate for them both—tall handsome strangers of noble rank would marry them, and their children would give them great joy until they slept the final sleep of peace surrounded by respectful children and their children's children. In a world where wonders of foresight were not easily dismissed, the ladies had respectfully repaid the fortune teller for her divination. For she proclaimed good news in a world too often troubled by the clashing waves of Norman and Saxon acrimony, of dog and underdog.

Though born on opposite sides of that divide, for many years they had been the best of friends, and many a day Marian would visit Ulrica at Torquilstone Castle where Ulrica's father Torquil, was its Saxon lord, or in turn been visited at Arlingford Castle where her father, Robert Fitz-Walter, was its Norman lord. The two girls had become as thick as thieves. So when Ulrica had suggested the gypsy's tent, Marian had followed as her shadow. It hadn't seemed a big deal.

Not all were happy with fortune tellers and their ilk, and the Mad Monk, outcast of Fountains and no longer a pure White Monk of the Cistercian Order, frowned upon the tent and the ladies who left giggling. He ponderously shook his heavy head. Still, girls will be girls, and the church had long been rather lax in her teaching. So it was not surprising that they knew no better, but he still felt a bubbling up of the spirit within him, almost to bursting point. Yet like a sheep is silent before its shearers, he opened not his mouth.

When he was not quiet he could be quite a controversial figure, ordained but unwanted by his brothers, gifted with the madness of mysticism. He lived on cold shoulder served up by his brethren, but then their monastic diet didn't suit his taste either. Neither did the occult fare of these ladies. Bah, what were crystal balls and such baubles to him, he who at times stood or sat as one spellbound, seeing sights and hearing words beyond the ken of mortal man? Why give the enemy a foothold? While loyal to the church his mother, he was saddened by her lack of engagement in spiritual warfare, and her all too frequent engagement in carnal warfare for earthly treasure. He went deeper in. In the world above—where many saw no more than a holy mother and her son—he had seen a loving father, a very disturbing vision, but a very captivating one.

Few monks read Scripture, for who needed its storyline once its wisdom had been distilled into systematic theology? But one day he had idly turned to its holy pages and found revelation beyond his wildest dreams and imagination. For instance he saw that the lord, although at Cana interceded to by the Blessed Virgin Mary to perform his first miraculous sign, had just before Calvary told the holy apostles that once he had died he himself wouldn't need to intercede for them. Why? Well, by the cross he would have made it possible for them to have direct access to God as their personal father and—here Brother Michael had sat back in his cell in fair amaze—the father would know and love them individually as children of his son's new creation, his new peoplehood.

The church didn't teach this: was God the forgotten father? Of course Michael still asked the holy mother to intercede, for holy mother church, founded by Saint Peter himself, had long taught that. But he was beginning to explore a strange new world in parallel to church dogma. This was one reason for his dubious reputation, the questioning of his orthodoxy. Yet weren't Church and Bible one?

Thereafter he had at times spoken directly to God as father, daringly though tentatively, as an explorer unsure about settling down on a rich volcanic plateau. Would he, as a peasant making themself at home in a king's palace, be damned for rank impertinence? For him—always in public and mostly in private—his prayer requests were to the Blessed Virgin, whom he believed would deliver them to her son, who in turn would speak to his father. It was a teaching of safety, for the church warned about the father's just severity, and who was Michael to naysay his mother? Those she cast out would be orphans cut off from salvation—*extra ecclesiam nulla salus*—and he lived by the back door. That was a good reason to bridle his tongue when his spirit begged to prophesy.

Yet this day his conscience troubled him yet again. Should he have warned these ladies about the dangers of the occult—even the pretence of the occult which so many fortune tellers represented as harmless fun? Would they not have pooh-poohed his fears? He knew full well that his reputation was often used against him, and that he was a bit of a bald Elisha within the church. He drew aside a while for quiet contemplation.

The afternoon was wearing thin. As the sun lowered he left the castle merriments. Untrue to form he lacked the jolliness of heart to partake of the festivities of that evening, when free bellytimber and rich ale would be provided by the lord of the castle to all and sundry, and jesters and jugglers would jubilantly entertain. His own mission was to reach, teach, and to entertain, but as the sun slowly set his spirit sunk low—had he failed to reach and teach? He stopped as the sun sank behind a thick cloud, portending a storm, and prayed alone and aloud for both ladies now long gone from his sight. Why were they on his heart? Why had he prayed in the spirit as dawn broke that very day, groaning incomprehensibly for their spiritual wholeness? Why had that great trinitarian, Gioacchino da Fiore, ever placed hands on him, beginning his visions into the unseen and prophetic burden?

Mindless of Wilfred of Ivanhoe, that evening Ulrica made her way alone, as the gypsy had advised, down to the old graveyard, where none now dwelt save some old bats in a cave. She had been told that she would meet the man of her dreams just beyond in the bridleway that ran alongside the same stream that fed the castle slightly above. Yes, it all sounded a little farfetched, but following the gypsy to the letter would test whether the woman had spoken true. Was the church, as her father believed, always right, or might some of the old bloodletting divinities of her Saxon people still have voices she should heed?

Yes, she had seen the Mad Monk shake his head disapprovingly at her and Marian, and she had thought him quite a fuddy-duddy. Why, he was despised and rejected by his own people of the cloth, so who was he to judge her! She had almost wished that he had come right out and given them a piece of his mind, for she would have given him a piece of her mind tit for tat. But no, rudeness would have saddened her dearest friend, Marian, and, well, it just wasn't right from a maid to a monk.

But as she walked away from both chaperone and shelter, she did feel just that little bit uneasy. "Fie on fear", she said to herself, doggedly quickening her pace to the old graveyard. The setting sun hid itself behind a dark cloud. A mournful breeze brushed past her as the dead murmurings of glacial ghosts in the air. She shivered from head to toe. She no longer heard the jovial sounds of laughter from within the castle, only the sad bubbling of the small waterfall.

Seldom had she walked alone, without at least a guard or two shadowing at a discreet distance. But the gypsy had said to go alone, else she would have warts for a husband, and so she had sneaked away in fear, hope, and suspicion. She was slowing up again. "Not far now, and anyway, there's probably no knight in shining armour really, and I can jolly well have the wench whipped as a mischievous miscreant, extorting money from us under false pretences! Though by now she's probably already packed her bags and scarpered with her ill-gotten gains. On the other hand...."

There was the graveyard, largely overgrown, a bit spooky really. But Ulrica wasn't the kind of young lady to be scared—or was she? It was after all getting a bit dim. Maybe she should give it up and go home for the night, or even to Cerdic's home as her crazy dream had urged. A number of Cerdic's people would return that evening from Torquilstone, and she always had an open invitation to stay anytime at Rotherwood, for its lord was a close friend of her family. "Ulrica, choose life and liberty, not death and domination. Turn from Darkness and unto the church, for therein is salvation." The voice of Michael! She slowly turned around, but no, no one was to be seen. A fanciful flashback to some half-heeded and less-needed sermon, doubtless. Almost there!

In the dell a stranger suddenly appeared in the fast approaching gloom, as if rising from a guileful grave. "Lady, I crave you mercy. I am forsooth a weary knight seeking lodgings for the night. Prithee point me on my way." Wow, he was absolutely gorgeous. Gypsy come back, all is forgiven! Ah alas, the paranormal can be seductively sweet when dressed up well.

"Sir Knight, this night my father would gladly give you bed and board. For he is the lord of Torquilstone Castle, just above us through this glade." She couldn't resist a grin, for she remembered how Cerdic of Rotherwood, a rather proud, fierce, jealous, and irritable man, had once said that hospitality should even be given to Jews, since, he had said, heaven having borne with that whole nation of stiff-necked unbelievers for more years than a layman could count, surely Saxon nobility should endure their presence for at least a few hours. Her own father had responded that in fact the true believers are the true Jews—but there, he had gotten some strange ideas into his head—such as his impending death—since he had turned to the church, even treating ethnic Jews, radical Muslims, and even dastardly Normans, as fellow children of Adam. Still, she loved him dearly. And this knight was as far above an ethnic Jew as Woden was above the Giants. She hoped that he would wish to stay many nights—how envious Marian would be!

"Gramercy, fair lady. I pray thee walk with me a while." And so saying he walked further from the castle and she, loth to let him walk alone, walked with him. The wind arose, and the rain began. He espied the nearby cave, and they hastened into it. "Tell me sweet one, what think you of the old religion?"

"Why sir, I am young, and my father has long forsaken it for the new, but I think that it still holds a power over the land. Are you Norman?" Oh pray don't say that you are of the crux religion.

"Norman? Nay, sweet lady. I am at loggerheads with them. Do you follow thy father or thine own heart? I must know." His unexpected intensity shook her somewhat. He was a strange man, even his language seemed to belong to a queer or quaint world, but he was so bewitchingly handsome. She felt her heart leading her on—was she getting in too deep above her head? But, she must answer truthfully.

"I would gladly know more of the old ways, such as my father's friends still hold to, but which he warns me not to seek." There, she had admitted to a complete stranger her inner defiance towards her father's catholic religion. Her father had not tried to convert her, but rather had lovingly allowed her to think it through for herself. "I think that God has no grandchildren, my daughter", he had said, meaning that each person could be a direct son or daughter of God, but could never be extended family.

That was mind boggling; that was so, well, unpagan-like. A well educated man, he believed that Judaics, Normans, Saracens, and Saxons, were all united in the *Imagodei*, and if heeding the new message could unite deeper in the *Imagochristi*—the message was the invitation. He was a patron of the controversial Mad Monk, who had inspired such radical ideas. Perhaps that was why she felt a little resentment towards the Mad Monk, challenging their tradition and preaching a unity between the oppressed Saxons and the oppressive Normans! She did not wish to love her neighbours if they were Norman—Marian was an exception but then Marian was Marian, a blend of both peoples and of Saxon mother.

"Then I will gladly show thee a way far older, my precious one. But behold, the rain has ceased, let us go hence into the castle, and beholden I shall be." And hence they went, and even as the Trojans had taken a horse tamely into Troy to their doom, so led the lady the knight into the hoary and ancient castle, a strong fortress though of no great size, with lower buildings overlooked by the great high square tower, encircled within an inner courtyard, and exterior wall surrounded by a water filled moat. Her father was delighted to lodge one of so fine a countenance and manner, more so at his daughter's request, for he would see her well wed, and Ivanhoe, on crusade to rescue the 'holy land' from the Saracen invaders, was from father estranged.

Many had perished on that righteous cause, for their king had preferred to fight than to win. But who was his guest? His name and, he said, his business, he would speak of fully on the morrow, and only great weariness prevented him from opening up long chapters too soon. As the dictates of hospitality demanded, he was forthwith taken to a guest chamber in the donjon, well above the nightly noises of the courtyard men at arms. Servants attended to his needs—which were few—and he was left to rest: so tired, it seemed, that he had even foresworn meat and mead, needing not the sleeping cup to sleep, that silver cup with its rich mixture of wine and spice.

But as the castle fell asleep he was if anything more awake. His inner diaboloi had been egging him on to a small-scale slaughter, unhappy that he had settled into a family that was generally content to feed itself on its petty little hates. He knew too well that he and his guests shared a compromise coexistence. They knew that if they pushed him too far he might disavow them, or be terminated by the queen as one who had jeopardised the veil of secrecy that secured her kingdom. They knew that if he died they would be homeless. On the other hand he knew that to refuse their pressure indefinitely would overthrow his mind intolerably.

So together they always slaughtered more than their host wished but less than his guests wished. In this spirit of compromise he had agreed to undermine this Saxon stronghold in exchange for enslaving the lady of the castle. Like a slender sylvan in summer, she was too fair to be felled. Here he was known as *Sir* Wulfgar. She would share his Darkness, though not so this night. The deed before him was distasteful to him, and he would return refreshed to the lady to take her to himself. Till then let the Front-de-Bœufs keep her safe. And that was his bargain for betrayal. But first he had had to meet her, to ensure that she was not faithful to the new religion, for such fidelity could pose problems for taking possession of her will. But she had assured him that it was safe, since she was not.

The festival had ended and the visiting merrymakers had returned to their homes. The drawbridge was up, and the guards patrolled silently save for muted greetings as they passed each other, clockwise and counterclockwise.

Suspicions had grown concerning the neighbouring Normans—those northern wolves from France—and the guards were on high alert, for easy would it be, and cheap, for Norman conqueror to justify to a Norman king his unjust aggression, on trumped up charge of treason. It was a silent and unholy night, when all was calm and the moon was bright, and Wulfgar quietly crawled down headfirst from his lofty room window.

First he dispatched the unguarded guards at the postern gate, then as arranged unlocked and lit the gateway with a torch. He who could have killed all neither wished to nor was permitted to do so by his inner guests—they revelled in human-against-human hostility. He merely guarded the open gate, ensuring that no guard would discover it being open to an enemy.

And so it was that, having used a floating bridge over the moat, the enemy swept in like a raging flood tide whipped up by the very breath of Usen. Torquil Wolfganger the Good and his seven valiant sons, defended their inheritance from story to story, but fell, and before their blood had dried, Ulrica's had been lost in the death of innocence, betrayed by her blindness. She wept, but Sir Wulfgar, long gone, knew neither of her weeping nor of its cause. Front-de-Bœuf had come and spoilt her house.

Seven   ғᴏʀᴇѕᴛ ᴏғ Hᴏᴘᴇ

These six years Ulrica had been lost to Marian, who still mourned her death. Oh that the king would return and put Britain to rights. When law becomes unjust, unlawfulness can be true justice. A depressing Darkness covered the land, but in the forest of Shirewude arose a beacon of Light, a true servant of the king, hope. And sitting under the jurisdiction of Baron William de Wendeval, the sheriff of Snotingham (later known as Nottingham), and the Priory of Saint Mary of Newstead, sat Papilwik, a gateway to the greenwoods. There there lived Marwolaeth, within hail of the Griffin and Saint James. As you might know, sometimes vampires change their names to throw off a sense of shame, and sometimes to fit into a different human culture—like changing clothes with changing fashions, or for local shortterm identities. Exiled here, she and her children had donned local aliases. In Papilwik she was familiar as Maudlin the 'Witch' of Papilwik, or plain old Mother Maudlin, with a daughter (some said granddaughter) named Docina, and a son (some said grandson), known as Lorell.

Where they had come from? They lived a secluded life in a hovel built alongside a cliff face, below which lay a dark and mysterious pool nestling below a cacophonous waterfall. Docina was worth more than a second look by any man not blind nor in dotage, yet no suitor dared to approach that hovel, for there was something intangible, invisible, intimidating, some unknown kind of unholy barrier. She would be neither romanced nor ravished. Lorell seemed a rather dashing young man, yet with a certain uncertainty of character displayed on his face.

Their mother—they called her that—was an old crone with a cracked voice. Yet the word was that she was a herbal healer of nocturnal habits, so was called upon at nights for healing purposes, such as bloodletting. For over a generation the church had stopped clergy from snicking veins, whether jugular, cubital, or femoral, but plenty of lay barber-surgeons had moved in to fill the gap—nature abhors a vacuum—trimming both hair and haima. Yet no barber was Maudlin. And her natural magic she said was only between her and her patients—most liked to leave it that way. They knew that magic was canny stuff to get involved with. She always visited the church at dusk, and you'd meet her, take her to the house of the sick, and then like a scalded cat scuttled away. Shirewude held many secrets.

Take Robin Hood, for instance. Always fearing pursuit his men hid caches of merchant garments and goods. Local villagers knew not where these caches were—nor wished to. The relationship between soldier, outlaw, and villager, was a balanced one. Often neither loved the others, but Robin's men were not of common outlaw kind which preyed on villages as wolves even as soldiers as lions sought out whom they might devour. No, Robin's men robbed only from the rich, and gave to the poor. Villagers in turn freely gave of what had not been forcibly taken. And whereas they would happily betray the wolf to the lion, few would happily betray Robin's men.

For one thing, hope of silver was often cheated. For another thing, their neighbours were often those these outlaws had helped—it didn't pay to fall out with your neighbours. And yet the villagers were under the thumb of the law, and to conceal known outlaws was a capital offence. Far better all around if help was for the most part kept under wraps. And *quid pro quo*, helping Robin's men was helping oneself, since Robin might return what the sheriff stole. Some villagers even—God knows it was precious little they could afford— put out food in wintertime, a time when many of Robin's men crept back into village life, some concealed as merchants, some concealed within their extended families. Giving succour to outlaws was *verboten*, but the villages scratched Robin's back—especially in winter—and he scratched theirs—especially in summer.

The local shepherds saw Robin as their hope and Marian—and who has not heard of her?—as their queen. Winter was harsh in the greenwoods—or say rather the bleak woods. You could fall to sleep in one world and awake in another. The wolf month did not help, when famished wolves forgot their fear of man. Robin was wise. Throughout the forest, winter supplies of nuts and berries were hidden. Some hollow trees made good larders—the holes were stopped up against squirrels and suchlike robbers. Even branch beds could be made off the beaten track where soldiers seldom trod, offering some raised protections against the frozen earth. Cold earth could lead to hypothermia, and men had gone crazy when exposed overly long to the elements, as heat drained from head to heart.

Enough winter food, protection, and warm horse leather jerkins and woollens—for the few who endured winter months in the forest—were essential, along with plenty to drink. And with wolves about a bit of fire didn't go amiss, either. Trouble was, there was always someone ready to capture or to kill Robin Hood.

Deep within the forest a trap had been sprung. Robert, nicknamed Robbing or just Robin, had been attacked by the sheriff. Soldiers had taken rolls of bark into the forest, wrapping them around tree trunks and around themselves. That was a new trick which some fresh faced young forester had come up with—he had called it a stakeout. It involved arresting some villagers—unable to pay their taxes—and publicly leading them away into that neck of the woods to be barbarously staked to nearby trees until they died by famine of by fiend. Robin had, as they had deliberately intended, heard of this new threat, and had had his spies in the village so that, when the tax collectors handed over some miscreants to the soldiers, the felons could be followed by friendly eyes.

Once the criminals had been staked out, most of the soldiers left, leaving just enough to warrant a strong force of outlaws to attempt the rescue: too few and the soldiers might contemptuously kill the prisoners first. Robin himself had led his merry men to the rescue, only to discover that covert soldiers far outnumbered their overt comrades. His men had put up a desperate fight against soldiers armed with crossbow and sword. After some loss they had managed to break out from the ensnaring circle, fleeing in different directions, each heading to locations where they could ditch sword, bow, and camouflage greens, and blend in in local villages.

It had been a hard run race, Robin every now and again turning to let loose an arrow with deadly aim, for these soldiers were so darned persistent. And no wonder, for the sheriff had offered both carrot and stick for the capture of Robin. Robin's own hardiness had meant that he had gained slightly on them, husbanding his strength for the uphill scramble. Thus it had been that they had followed him up more slowly, while he had gained yet more distance, working his way along the top of the escarpment, then down into the plains and unto the shepherds. Time enough to change and camouflage himself as a sheep among the shepherds of Woolsthorpe.

And it had worked. The few soldiers who had gingerly clambered down the steep slopes had not spotted him, for he was wrapped in a coat of sheep's wool and concealed within the large flock, sheep unafraid of human kind among them. Curiously Robin had always had an affinity with shepherds, having been born on Monday the seventh day of January in the year of our lord, 1157, Christmas Day for the Eastern Orthodox under Julian. Christmas, the official birthday of the *Agnes Dei*, a day when shepherds had visited the house of Saint Joseph's parents in Bethlehem to worship and convince his parents of the child's holy origins, gaining honourable lodging for the holy family, who in disgrace had been denied the guest room.

And even as in those days—when what had been the Holy Land had known turmoil and wanhope yet hope had come through a birth—so too in times of turmoil and wanhope had Robin been born in the depths of Shirewude. For his high born parents had married in secret. This had come about because Joanna his mother had been daughter of Sir George Gamwell, Saxon, and William Fitz-Ooth his father had been son of the Baron of Kyme, Norman. Sir George had never forgiven the Norman invaders, and had threatened death to the wooer of his daughter.

Yet her heart and hand were given to William, and he had visited her at nights as her husband until she was too heavy with child to deceive her father any longer. At that point, aided by her husband she had fled his halls, and her father had pursued until, discovering her in the greenwood nursing her newborn, he had forgiven her husband for his grandchild's sake. Believing that the place of his birth had been by fate, his parents had brought Robert up in its ways, developing a sense of justice, chivalry, and self-reliance within him. Now he was a hunted man—as his father had been.

It was hard now to imagine that only a few years ago, Robert Fitz-Ooth had been discovered to be the true Earl of Huntingdon. For both his family tree, and the written and substantiated confessions left with monks—by Judith and her daughter Matilda and only to be revealed after their deaths—had of late come to light in a remarkable chain of events. Better late than never, though usually better never late. The old and ancient documents had only been unearthed by events connected to the accession to the throne of Richard, son of Henry 2, in 1189.

It was welcome news to Richard, too, for he had had mixed dealings with Dauíd of Scotland, Earl of Huntingdon and friend of Richard's brother John, and was predisposed to dispossess Dauíd of his title. And he made it abundantly clear that if Dauíd stirred up trouble for the son of William Fitz-Ooth, then Richard himself would swiftly denounce Dauíd with a charge for high treason. Dauíd had cannily given way under such duress, knowing that the false evidence against him would be damning, and unwilling to give credence to such falsity by rising up in arms against Richard. So he quietly conceded the point of inheritance and relinquished his title.

He knew full well that there was more than one way to skin a cat, and if Robert Fitz-Ooth could be assassinated or otherwise undermined, well, there seemed no other claimant to the earldom. It should simply revert to Dauíd and history might overlook the hiccup. But wrongly did Dauíd suspect that Richard had forged the 'unearthed' testimonies. Thus it was that under Richard, the son of Joanna Gamwell had repossessed the ancestral title of Earl of Huntingdon, bringing to it his Saxon sympathies. Moreover, brought up with a wooden rather than a silver spoon, he was one with commoners and offered Norman hope to the Saxon hopeless.

And that is why, even after Prince John had abruptly outlawed Robert on a trumped up charge, the people of Shirewude still affectionately called him their Robin, Earl of Huntingdon and Lord of Locheslei. The latter had been his parental home, unjustly yet legally stolen by Sir Guy of Gisborne, sworn lover of the Lady Marian and therefore mortal enemy of his rival Robin. Sir Guy had taken much from Robin. His home; Robin had moved to the forest's roof. His cattle and swine; Robin switched to the king's deer. His money; Robin became the robber's robber. But Sir Guy had never taken the lovely Maid Marian, whose affection for Robin knew no bounds. They had long been sweethearts, and he her idol ever since her carefree days with her long deceased friend Ulrica, for whose soul she still prayed for every Thursday.

Their wedding at Fountains had been cut short, but he and his wife respected the sacramental customs of the day and had graciously vowed celibacy until either Marian's father or King Richard himself blessed their full wedding. Besides, a child would tie them down in days that needed them to be free: so too had Saint Paul, their hero and lover of women, deprived himself of marriage for the good of his mission. Robin was a man to inspire much affection from the poor in pocket, and from the holy of heart. Feared by the bad, he was loved by the good. Now the affection from the common people had paid off yet again, and Robin had once more escaped John's unjust law.

Long helped by these shepherds of Belvoir Vale, in thanks Robin invited them to meet him and his merry men at Papilwik. Weeks later, leaving undershepherds to tend the flocks, many had gathered before dawn at Scrimshire Lane, Cots' Grave, a little south of the old burial ground, setting out together and passing through Nottingham's Backside, then through Basford Waste and Dorket Head. Of their number Karolin, himself born in Papilwik, had journeyed the day before and had not returned. He had reconnoitred to check that the party had neither been rescheduled nor rerouted, so not returning was good news.

As they walked they fervently prayed that Robin would one day take back his ancestral titles, yet they still felt honoured guests of an earl and his lady. Little did they expect that the party would be the surprise it would be, touching things beyond the veil of human experience, but shepherds were no strangers to surprise. Had not a shepherd once seen a burning fire within an unburning bush? Had not a young shepherd with a sling once slain a giant? Had not backwater shepherds once seen visitors to our world as a heavenly choir, and lived to tell the tale?

Eight   Hoodwinked

The shepherds arrived at the Griffin on the appointed day in June, mixing a little with other travellers just to be sociable, but keeping their business to themselves. By certain signs and countersigns they touched base with members of Robin's band, who after checking them out left along the road to the Raven's head and the Fish pool, and Mamesfeld market. In dribs and drabs the shepherds followed. Once all were following the vanguard, a rearguard of Robin's people stealthily watched the Griffin to ensure that none were tracking them. All was clear, and speedily catching up with the vanguard they helped direct the shepherds along meandering paths in the woods. Whether or not it was to Thieves Wood that they went, this story does not tell. Suffice to say that they were courteously greeted by Robin himself, along with his spiritual advisor Michael Tuck and his special bodyguard Little John.

"Hail, Robin", said Lionel.

"Greetings Lionel, but what of our friend Eglamour? How comes he not to be here for our merry meeting?" asked Robin, showing his apprehension, fearing that somehow mishap had been his lot.

"Alas, as we crossed the Trent his betrothed ran from us we knew not why, but we waited a while by the bridge. When we sought her out, she was nowhere to be seen. We were not expected, so it is unlikely that robbers lurked there, and surely we would have heard her cry had she met with any by the waters. No, for my part I think it all too clear that whether she went to empty or to fill herself by the water's edge, that she ventured upon a slippery slope and there met her fate under the waters, hitting head against stone. Eglamour was in shock, but said that the earl awaited us, and 'twould be disrespectful to keep our lord awaiting for the loss of but one sheep. At his bidding we left him searching downstream for her body. Yet he begged that you would forgive him any offence for being absent from your table this day, and that by your grace he would seek for days by water, wood, and wold, in some hope that she wanders witless." With that Lionel bowed low, his cap in hand.

"Dear Eglamour, does he not know that I care for him and his as for my own, and for the fair Earine would hasten myself with my men in search of her or her body?" Robin looked prepared to do just that, but Lionel begged him on Eglamour's behalf to continue with the feast, for, he said, Eglamour would be sadder to have caused its loss. At that moment Maid Marian arrived with men carrying parts of a red stag-deer for the party. As the custom was, the Raven's Bone had been given to a raven which had shadowed them, but Karolin had had a bad feeling about that bird. Marian had wondered whether it lived with some villagers, since she had noticed some green thread tied around one leg. But putting all that aside, they had gaily proceeded to the rendezvous point, Marian, too buoyed with having beaten Scarlett to the kill, failed to sense the sadness in the air.

"Welcome me with thanks, Robin, for by my arrow I bring my gift to this festal time. But what is the matter my love?" she quickly asked, for she saw that her jollity was not reflected in Robin's face. "Is any hurt?" Briefly she was told, and briefly she wept. But she had known much pain and loss, and so could soon wipe tears away—genuine tears for all that. Now she would also pray on Thursdays for the soul of Earine, for she believed that souls in purgatory were there under God's blessing, being purged of all rags of sin until able to approach the majesty on high in pure robes of righteousness.

∞

Mother had been called upon to heal a patient. As was her wont she had visited the church with the setting of the sun. There a villager awaiting her had, by way of pleasing her—for she always enquired for news when her services were sought—told her that she had that very evening overheard Karolin, a shepherd born and bred there but taken up service with the castle in Belvoir Vale, tell his parents that that morrow Robin of Locheslei was to hold a feast for shepherds of the Vale, and that Marian Fitz-Walter would be joining them, met and led by Karolin himself at early dawn.

Fate would have flowed otherwise had this earwigging blabbermouth not delighted in her scoop. She, proud talebearer, had left, leaving Maudlin to treat the patient, but that night she had done so with less than her usual diligence, for her mind had turned to darker matters. She soon returned to her hovel in cogitation. Should she report Robin's whereabouts to the Sheriff of Nottingham to have him hanged? Too simple; too short. No, curse him with pain and longevity, to die a broken old man, not a brave young one. She hated human marriage—why not stick to mating?—yet to turn their desire into disaster would make their haplessness her happiness: Robin's years of tears should not be cut short.

But first: "Lorell, the road between here and there must be watched. Study the shepherds as they come. May they whom the heir of Walleff has summoned as shield, pierce his soul as sword! Make them venture through a valley of Baka; make them weep, so that he weeps with them." Lorell quickly took up the commission. No love had been lost between him and Grindan, but as a dog of war he loved to be let loose to cry 'havoc' as a terrier among rats, so as to quieten his guests who now were baying for blood. Besides, a son was to be dutiful to his mother, at least if the duty was to himself.

Although he did not enjoy the sunshine, he could still tolerate its dimness if mixed with shadows, at least for short periods. So it was that he had soon picked up the trail of the shepherds as they walked in the early morning light towards the river. From the trees he had studied their relationships, planning what to do. A shepherdess had attracted his evil eye. That she was the wife or almost the wife of the chief shepherd seemed clear, and that she could become the slave-bride of Lorell himself also seemed clear to him. Whether his new mother would let him keep her was unknown, but at the very least she would let him bleed her. And stealing her while they travelled to party with Robin would certainly cause Robin grief, perhaps even turn them against the heir of Walleff. That could be useful.

So it was that Lorell went ahead of them and lurked near the bridge they must cross. Thus it was that he appeared to Earine as a lamb in a trap, its bleats sounding telepathically only in her ears, so that she and only she turned quickly off the road to rescue it. Then it was that he caused her to faint, and in human form deftly carried her away out of sight, until all but one of the shepherds had crossed over. Then he crossed over, carrying her expeditiously through cover of woodland by best possible speed, straight to the grotto where he lived. Mother had seemed quite pleased with his contribution to the pack, but more inclined to skin her alive than to have Lorell slave-marry her.

For Lorell, beauty counted much, but his mother objected that Earine was too lowborn to be of much use in intelligence gathering. She had an eye for business not for beauty; for use not for ornament. Besides, had she not already lost a son by needless dalliance with a damsel, though at least *she* might have been useful. Let meat be for meat, not for marriage even if only slave-marriage. To be a rock, an island, is to never cry, but the truth was that Lilith had already excommunicated this family, and excommunication was sometimes eased by human companionship as a pet, and Lorell was feeling the pinch. Nor perhaps was Docina totally immune.

Docina had been sent to spy on the Lady Marian, by way of Karolin, and she saw her setting forth from Arlingford as a shepherdess alongside the shepherd and one or two whose garments blended in with the trees. As a raven she had pursued them since the crack of dawn, watching their hunt for game, and stalked them even as they stalked the stag. It was with suspicion that the shepherd's eye had spotted her. Before the dawn she had on a whim visited the shepherd, awaking his unease unwisely, perhaps. For as he had slept in his parents' hut, she had whispered words of doom in his ears, whispered the family curse on those befriending the one doomed to die.

Why had she done that, she wondered? To cause him pain, or to save him from it? It is a fact that to be cut off from the Night is to stir up *sehnsucht*, a deep inconsolable longing for the other, for an I-Thou relationship, for the unfound flower briefly scented. Prisoners in isolation can even turn to rats as to companions—or else suffer madness. The world of noise often protects from such feelings, but in her silence she had experienced a sudden distasteful wave of inner doubt, before rapidly returning to reality. Well, so what if Karolin now deemed her to be a bird of a different feather—what could he do to thwart her? Perched aloft, she continued to watch.

It was only after the killing of the stag and its butchering, that, swooping to collect the Raven's Bone, she departed to her home, for she was in no hurry to harry the hunted. Her mother was pleased with her news, for her lithe mind quickly conceived a plan: the stag party should put the fox among the hen party. The Raven's Bone was quickly turned into brew and stew. Vampires need no substance other than the blood they convert by their spirit-power into bodily substance, on which their earthly life now depends, but they can enjoy food and drink—for pleasure, not for permanence. And their captive needed feeding until they agreed upon its fate. Little did they perceive the watchful eye of Karolin, who, forewarned of their dwelling place, had followed the raven's flight. Even now he wasn't sure, but there was at least less unsureness in his mind as he stole away.

Maudlin was watching and waiting. She had allowed Marian to deliver the venison to the cooks, and then as expected leave to freshen up after both hunt and hack. It was then that Karolin returned. "Karolin, the Lady Marian has told me of your fears about Maudlin the Witch. Tell me, are such tales about her true or but jest?" enquired Robin.

"In truth, not in jest, good master. Indeed I fear that she even now watches us, for I was warned in a dream to have nothing to do with you lest I share in your doom. And the raven, if raven it was, took the bone to Maudlin, unless it was she herself, for many suspect her to be a shapeshifter. Is it so strange that tragedy has already overtaken us? Or am I not right to fear that Maudlin the Witch chooses more than a bone to chew on—that very bone I saw being broiled in her camp?" warned Karolin. Robin held his head in hand, pondering what it might mean, and what he should do. At that moment Marian returned— seemingly.

"Witch? You simpleton; you fool. How dare you, a baseborn peasant, call my friend names? She is wise; does that make her a witch? Shame on your pathetic bleating, scabby sheep! And you dare come here begging for food from my hand? How now could I give rich meat to ignorant ingrates who deserve no more than a starved sheep's carcase?" Marian's face was cold yet enraged. All were taken aback by such a change in her countenance and courtesy.

"Marian my love," implored Robin, "these good folk have befriended me often and saved my life. Becalm yourself, pray, or do you speak thus in jest my sweet?"

"Saved your life? Yes indeed, but such a life as had to bleat within a flock of fellow sheep. Is that a life worth saving? You fled nobly from mere soldiers, you who claim still the earldom! You who now welcome even the worship of shepherds? Why has Norman lady shackled herself to one so sunken from riches to rags, fit only to sleep with sheep? You who bethinking himself a shepherd keep spy on my every movement, lest I stray? So, swill your ale with this riff-raff peasantry, but the stag is mine.

Scarlet, you are witness that by my hand the noble beast fell, now do as I bid and take it to my true friend Maudlin in token of my high esteem of her. Go now!"

At a nod from Robin, Will Scathlock took back the stag, and with some others took it in the direction that Marian indicated, knowing that they must follow the stream to its pooling. Marian turned her back on Robin and departed in a huff, leaving Robin with tears in his eyes. "Friends," said he, "forgive I pray thee both my lady and myself, for merrymaking is no longer in my heart. I fear that some madness has possessed her, and I must catch her up and discover what ails her." So saying he walked as a dead man to the stream that Marian had headed to, slowly for he was half fearful of the meeting. At last he spotted her alone. "Marian. What has come over you? Why have you called me jealous and oppressive? Why have you insulted our guests? And why have you taken this Mother Maudlin as friend?" he sternly demanded as she stood smiling sweetly at the water's edge. He was confused, caring, and cross.

"My love, what nonsense is this? Why are you teasing me so?" she asked, both puzzled and alarmed.

"Deny it not, for all heard you. Even now the stag is sent to Mother Maudlin at your command, since in your eyes our guests are unfit for it." Will Scathlock had returned, for Mother Maudlin's hovel was not far distant, and hearing the news from the camp had hurriedly followed where Robin had gone. Stopping short, he stood silently by, pondering.

"But Robin, I commanded not but that our honoured guests should feast upon it. Scarlet, if you have taken it elsewhere, do by all which is holy bring it back as sent in error. Oh Robin, why are you upsetting me so with such folly?" said she tearfully. Minutes and still more minutes passed in bitter silence. There seemed no more words to be said. Robin was seeking to drive her insane, but what had she done to deserve it?

At which point Amie the gentle shepherdess approached and, apprised of the conflict, hastened to testify that she had left the camp with Marian, who had sought out the stream to wash and refresh herself, and they had been chatting there until Amie had discreetly left on seeing her lover approach. Amie herself had been earlier kissed, and had subsequently experienced feelings new to her. She who had wished to ask Marian if she was suffering from a heart disease, now defended her friend from heart disease: Marian couldn't have been talking with Robin in the camp *at the same time* as talking with her at the stream! She had heard of second personalities, but never of second bodies! It was at that point that Mother Maudlin herself appeared, an old driggle-draggle with a crackly voice, thanking Marian for the gift, rubbing it in.

"But good mother, Scarlet gave it to you in error. I beg you to forgive, for it must be for our special guests who have come this long way for festal celebration", pleaded Marian.

"Then alas, sweet mistress," replied Maudlin, "for many poor neighbours came just now to my camp, and in the goodness of my heart I gave away all of the stag. Your friends will surely understand my mistake, even as I understand and forgive your jest on a poor old crone", chuckled Maudlin.

Breathless, Scathlock ran back to the stream. "Good master, the stag is returning to our camp, so the party may turn into a feast yet."

"What!" exclaimed Maudlin with a shriek, "you dared to enter my home and steal my meat, you harecop bespawler? Fie on you thief!"

"But Mother Maudlin, how could we steal from your camp what you have given away from your camp? And surely you would not claim as yours what you have given to others? Nay, it must be that as your neighbours have been blessed by your bounty, so we here have now been blessed by some unknown bounty, some unknown stag. And so we must both be grateful, must we not?" said Marian with a smile, outfoxing the fox.

Maudlin stormed away uttering curses on camp and cook enough to turn one's blood cold, some of which she could bring to pass by her telekinetic power—what simpletons called spells. With her departure their minds were cleared. Robin had long known that a generational curse hovered over the House of Walleff. He also brought to mind that Karolin had briefly spoken of a curse heard haunting his dreams. Might it be that the line of Maudlin had long harried the line of Matilda, once presumed daughter-Heir of Walleff, dividing his family tree? Walleff had killed a shapeshifter, and had not a shapeshifter not taken the guise of Marian?

But why? To steal a stag? Ridiculous! But what might have happened? His wife had seemingly gone mad. It might well have been that a rift would have widened between him and her, perhaps she would have ended up locked away for lunacy or in a nunnery where spiritual power was thought able to keep madness in check. Was that it? Was the curse being shaped to make him suffer her loss, and—he would neither divorce her nor take another while she lived in the body—to die childless?

Maudlin! There were some kind souls who prayed for her, believing that in spite of her good works she was by fiend enthralled. Soon she would depart, and many years later Reuben, one of Robin's men of failing memory, would recall that just before she did she had seemed repentant, and thus a strange story arose of her having been joyously reconciled to heaven. But prayers had not been answered. They of Papilwik understand neither her real nature nor her destiny, but it is said that love tries to believe the best.

Yet the facts are otherwise. The real Maudlin returned home in a rage. Her children looked apologetic. Scathlock and other armed outlaws had ventured into their camp, seized the venison, and retired in triumph. Either child could have ripped all to pieces, but they were already under the watchful glare of Lilith who had confined them to live in the greenwood, threatening death if they revealed their true identifies and power. So feigning weakness they had had to watch helplessly, fearing that Maudlin's plan was coming apart. The meat itself was a side issue. To Maudlin, slight hope remained that Robin would further question Marian's sanity, but slight hope was better than no hope, and she might sow further seeds of doubt through shapeshifting. And there was still a tasty morsel awaiting within, a nice crumb of comfort.

Eglamour had been found weeping and wailing in the woods, and been gently led to Robin's camp. He had finally given up hope of finding Earine's body, and his mind had moved from madness to melancholy. For reclothed in his right mind he had realized that had she fled from some vile outlaw into the woods, she would have cried out for help, and would not have fled away from help. But if surprised by such a villain she might easily have panicked and slipped into the fast running river and failed to cry out. But by hook or by crook drowned she must have been. He now stood sorrowfully at Robin's side.

"Marian", asked Robin, "what was it you once told me about a dream your friend Ulrica had about she and you? That very day she perished with her father for tarrying at Torquilstone? Of you she said that you would die well without children, did she not? So far we await a wedding pleasing to your father, and hope to welcome Richard. I wonder whether the witch has tried to part us, which would be barrenness indeed. Do you think that it was she who planted this dream within the heart of Ulrica, my dear?"

"I think not, Robin. Since the dream warned her, was it not against, not from, the witch? And it bespoke my barrenness as a blessing, not a curse, though I confess a blessing I find hard to bear, for I would that we had child born in this wood even as were you, beloved. And I fear becoming another's bride, the more as I fear Sir Guy—you I waited long to marry, and would not part from now", replied Marian.

"Yet the witch is at work, nonetheless. See how she has sought to raise conflict between us, to change our love to loathing. She is a deceiver, and a murderess. For it seems to me that the loss of Earine was by her hand, an arrow to wound me as the true target of her vendetta. Drowned by her craft, unless.... Little John, I think there is not a moment to lose. Go swiftly to the witch's cottage and.... Eglamour!" cried Robin. For Eglamour had suddenly cried out to his lost love and fled into the wood. What witchcraft was upon them? But then as clear as day he and Marian saw the slender form of Earine haring away through the trees. "By Mother Mary 'tis her or her ghost or, or.... Little John, swiftly now to Mother Maudlin's, and keep sharp eye on her until I come.

Beware of her magic" warned Robin. With Little John commissioned Robin sped off in pursuit of Eglamour, fearing lest the woman, wraith, or witch, led him to harm. He knew not that it was Docina—neither woman, wraith, nor witch, but vampire—commanded by her mother to rekindle false hope in the breast of Eglamour, reflexive pain for Robin.

Robin was swift, but Eglamour was swifter still, leading Robin a wild goose chase, until Robin lost sight of the goose. Precious minutes he searched the ground for tracks, but none met his eyes. Lingering in indecision he heard the cry of Little John's horn. "Alas, Little John in danger? Is this day bewitched?" And veering off he abandoned Eglamour to his uncanny fate and tore towards the witch's grotto, there to find an astonishing sight.

For there was Little John, Eglamour (just arrived), and Marian, whom he had left with Amie in the camp. And not even a breathless Marian, but a Marian who had just been telling Little John to return to Robin. Robin's pursuit had been swift, had veered only slightly away from the cottage, and had been quite a distance. Even he was fairly breathless and hot. Yet there was Marian as cool as a cucumber, or as like to Marian as two peas in a pod. Except that was for a thin green cord around her waist. "Good Marian, what of Mellifleur with whom I left you?" asked he.

"Dearest Robin, I invited her to visit with me, but she felt too tired" Marian replied.

"You have run so well today that you have outpaced me, Marian, and yet are as fresh as a daisy, as I think Amie was when I left you two alone."

The false Marian had looked to run as soon as she had clapped eyes on Robin. Now discovered in the lie she darted towards the hovel, but Robin darted quicker, managing to grab her green sash as she dived through the doorway. Immediately the old crone Maudlin appeared from within. "You have broken my sash, robber of women. Call yourself a man? Give it back this instant" screeched Maudlin.

"Why, good mother, did it not come from my own true lady love? How now do you claim it?" She answered not but stood glaring at him. "I guess this is some magic cord, some charm of witchcraft." And so saying he flung it into the churning cauldron. "Begone from your hovel within five minutes, for if not we shall see how you are shaped by arrows." As he spoke several of his men appeared, who had also heard the horn of Little John. Maudlin and her family could have dispatched them in the bat of an eye, yet dared not vex Lilith further. Maudlin looked to the pool. Fool, the cord could be found and fixed—it was still useful.

Her family too had such cords of power, into which they had siphoned off something of their energy, batteries allowing boosts of energy at need, though the need was seldom. The weaves were of their own substance, a craft beyond the lot of man and seldom used by vampires. Witch, she was called, but she cared not. It was safer that they think her thus, than to know her true nature. If they banished her as a witch, Lilith would understand and grant her dwelling elsewhere. If she stood her ground these fools would swiftly die, but Lilith's judgement could spell instant death.

At her call Lorell and Docina came forth. They had listened from within, and were prepared to depart, indeed with glowing torches seemed prepared to burn down their small cottage—though Lorell seemed somewhat hesitant. But Robin, arrow on the string, caused them to wait until he had explored their hut. "Good mother, you would surely have grieved to leave without showing us such a treasure, a treasure none would have buried and none should burn", he scorned, as he came out leading Earine by the hand. She had been kept within bound hand and foot and gagged. The audacity of them, that they would have murdered her under her friends' very noses.

Well, they did not deserve to live, and though Robin had never killed a woman in his life he burned to do so in this case. Punishment is justified when the punished deserve it, and if not capital can sometimes be remedial, helping to prevent the offender from re-offending, making them face if not their own sin at least their fear of future punishment, besides acting as a deterrent to others who might similarly offend. Here was a murderous family, which seemed to have it in for him and his. "Tell me witch, why has your family hounded mine, for are you not of they who cursed my forebear Walleff for killing he who sought to steal away his sister? The telling of that tale is confused, I doubt not, but that he and the bat were one—as he who was my father did tell—at last seems credible to me. For if shape shifting there was, I can believe that you are born of that stock", he sternly said. It was no time for faffing about and beating around the bush.

"Good Robin," cried Maudlin, grovelling abjectly at his feet, "please spare a poor old crone and the children of her poverty. I confess that my mother was a witch like me, as hers before her. But they were treated harshly without mercy. I have wronged you, but no harm has been done, the saints be praised. I have called you names, but forgive my foolish rudeness, noble sir. To err is human. As for the woman my lad took, he was but lonely without wife. I told him to let her loose, but he is such a forceful young man. My playful children made but jest to burn the house with her inside—no harm would have come to her, I swear. For their sins I promise you they will be sent to monastery and nunnery to repent and learn better ways. And from the goodness of my heart I have been a healer to the poor people of Papilwik."

And so it was that she lied lie upon lie, declaring virtues and denying vices. Robin doubted her veracity, but being loth to take human life unless needful, and willing to give them the benefit of the doubt, he chose to spare not slay, and in sparing he was spared not slain. "Then go quickly with your lives, but if you remain long in sight we will hunt you like wolves, and if ever we see you in Shirewude you will be killed as a wolf. Pray to Our Lady that your leopard spots will be changed." Mother Maudlin had pulled, or thought that she had pulled, the wool over his eyes, and could gracefully withdraw without incurring the wrath of Lilith.

Mercy was not always affordable, and Robin was not always merciful. In fact he could be as barbaric as his barbaric times required, slaying those who had no sword but could point the sword in his direction. Yet by the codes of the time he and his merry men were also honourable, and this time good fortune favoured his mercy, mercy he might have regretted had he known something of its results. For although with her departure the curse lifted as a mist from Robin— for a time—it also signalled the return of Lorell to poor Ulrica, hidden far from reach and rescue.

But for now the party could make merry. Earine had returned as from death, and indeed she had been close to the winter death of the soul, or to the eventide death of the body. And Eglamour had had plans for new life, joining his body with hers with Brother Michael as chief witness to their commitment of union. And once Amie had been kissed, with Marian's enlightenment her heart had quickly warmed to new emotions, so that when her new found lover proposed that since one wedding was to take place, another should too, she had readily agreed.

The party would end on a far happier note than it had begun, celebrating goodwill between outlaws and shepherds. For these herders of sheep, sadness was banished that day.

"Brother Tuck," asked Lionel, having summoned Tuck aside, "forgive me I pray, but one thing puzzles me about you and Robin. We shepherds are often fleeced by the law, and Robin's outlaws have saved us and have never stolen from us, so our bond I understand fully. But, if you do not mind my asking, how can it be that being of the church you are happy to serve outlaws? In short, should the church support law or outlaws?"

"Good shepherd," replied Tuck, "how is it that you support even the hundredth sheep that strays? Say rather that in these days the ninety nine stray even more, and with them I find I must use rod more than staff. The holy apostle told they of Rome—of that mighty city of ungodly power—that God had anointed lawmaking which was to be obeyed, but hastened to add that that support was but to laws that maintained peace and justice for the common weal. As with them, with us. But when lawmakers make laws to enrich themselves or in obedience to idols, do they not rather make themselves outlaws to the law of God, and might then the outlaws they persecute be the lawful of God, offering true obedience to God's absolute law, rather than to man's relative law? So it is with godly Robin. Tainted with sin as are we all, yet sinned against by they who hold the power of tyranny. So we should pray the more for those in authority over our land, that they may use true wisdom within their limited remit from above. Thus it is that Robin awaits the return of the king, as one awaits God's anointed."

"Brother Tuck, I think I understand. Under good law an outlaw must be bad, but under bad law an outlaw might be good. But bethink you that we shall have good law with the return of Richard?" asked Lionel.

Tuck lowered his voice. "Lionel, such questions are unwise, and should not be sounded in Robin's ears, for in innocence he has set much store on our king. Yet by your words and tone I perceive that you have heard disturbing rumours of Richard, as have I. This third Crusade was aimed to deliver Jerusalem from Saracen hands, yet it is said that the Lion squeezed the armies into his will, and that his will was to fight rather than to free, for he is at heart a fighting lion—and has he turned a just war into an unjust? He has fought father, mother, brothers, wife, and even pope and allied kings. And, though every time Richard did put the crusaders into action—of siege, march, skirmish or open battle—the Saraceni lost or retreated, yet by ignoring the plight of Jerusalem was he not Saladin's greatest friend? This I fear is the Lion who was captured by crusaders who were sided with the pope—though by imprisoning a king disloyal to the pope, became themselves disloyal to the pope. Alas, a king who subverts the very spirit of crusades!

"However it will be if the Lion returns to our shores, we must still seek his return, for otherwise we side against constitution and with civil war. For good and ill he unites us as our anointed king. But to what extent is a monarch under God? Godly King David had been anointed, but what of ungodly King Ahab? Pagan King Cyrus had been anointed, but what of pagan King Achaemenes? Were David and Cyrus the most moral of messiahs? Even if godly anointing gave godly advantage in that age, does it in ours? And what evidence is there for monarchs today being deificly anointed, and that if they are, of them always being godly? All had sinned, my humble friend. It grieves me that some babblers still contend—and that with windy eloquence—that kings are not to be numbered among the laity, since they have been anointed with priestly oil.

"But these windbags do not see that since kings—and what of queens?—are not numbered among the clergy, and since all (save monks—who have neither wife nor sword) are either clergy or laity, then kings have to be laity. And since few kings can read the Holy Vulgate, let alone do so, we might even say *rex illiteratus est asinus coronatus*! But let us hope for the best." Tuck bowed his head: the church had shown the world heavenly light, but alas both church and crown were still far from ideal, sunken perhaps.

The good Brother seldom stayed long in melancholy, especially when venison pie remained for supper, and good weddings awaited his beneficence. So it was that soon he and Lionel were returned to the gay party, eating and drinking with the best. As the sun lowered in the skies, he blessed the marriages of both happy couples, joined them in a parting cup, and waved adieu to the shepherds as they returned for the night to the Griffin. Little did he know that, in an ignominy so vile that compared to it death was but sweet sorrow, Ulrica yet lived. And little did any foreknow that, though twitted for now, the family of Maudlin would wreak further vengeance on Robin and his house.

For so it would be that Richard would return and Robin, restored to earldom, would be fully wedded to Marian thus a maid no more. And that was pure joy. Yet all too soon Richard would again leave the land uneasy, and within five years word of Richard's death would come first to Prince John, that cunning fox which would seek the heads of Robin and Marian. Records of Robin's earldom would be irrevocably effaced by King John, although one wishful account, erring that he was born when he was three, erred also in saying that it began at Robin's birth and lasted until Marian's death in 1247 *anno domini*: oh that it had been so.

Robin would escape to the sea; Marian to a nunnery. Seeking the yellow root of evil, a prioress of Kyrkesly would turn Marian into nun and—inspired by a visiting Sister Docina—seeking safety, would hand Robin unto death. Yet it was destined that he who would be merciful unto her would die in the arms of his wife, and that their very bodies would lie together, two mounds made into one, until they were no more—and long was their mound sacred. And before her time came, Marian, that 'bride of Christ', superseded the prioress and let the light of the priory shine unto the poor and needy, showing by the good that it did, the praise of the father of heaven. Her head was thus exalted in honour, fulfilling the personal prophecy long spoken in Ulrica's vision. But no child did she bear in the flesh.

Robin freed; vampires enslave. Mercy is a hard lesson for an unbeliever. For Wulfgar, the question of freedom would be its testing point, but that point lay in the unseen future. Mercy, as far as he was concerned, was a counterintuitive lesson, which could prove fatal if fully learnt. He had been told that it was a bitter lesson that left an unpleasant taste in the mouth, a taste only washed away by blood. It was certainly one he neither expected nor wished to learn. Robin had cost him a bird in a bush, but he would not cost him the bird in his hand.

Ulrica! Six long weary years on from teenage folly, when she had gaily spread the welcome mat before Wulfgar. Torquilstone's dark tower once more sank into the oblivion of night. On a day best forgotten, its steps and courtyard had been deeply stained with noble and pure blood, and in peace it would not die. Many times since then, shrieks and groans of yet more victims disturbed its uneasy slumbers, and its roots of muddy moat were strewn with bodies of the unborn—for men would hide their faces from the unwanted fruit of their shameful seed sown in sin. Guilt shrouded it now in its unquiet sleep of dishonourable dotage—would no pyre rid the world of it? Within its chambers lay Ulrica, daughter of Torquil Wolfganger the Good, granddaughter of Ingolf the Wise, great-granddaughter of Herleif the Just, and great-great-granddaughter of Torquil Wolfganger the Builder, Ulrica the Forgotten. Ulrica, slave of the usurper to whom women were but toys to amuse his playful hours.

The deceiver had returned, seemingly now to take his turn. Ulrica lay helpless and hopeless before him. "Gramercy, fair lady. I pray thee lay with me a while." Shivering, her head under threadbare blanket, cold lips hovered over her long dead face, red eyes in the dark punishing her defiant will to live. Mockingly, as a cat to a mouse, they moved past her wet cheeks to her bare dry neck. Her hands tightened on the sheet as the mouth hesitated, as unseen teeth were bared. Pain, sharp stabbing pain, suffused her brain, as he bit into her. Trying to remember her life before death, her neck felt a trickle of warm blood, and her ears heard his sigh of relief as he drew life from her very veins.

He was different, more terrifying, than the men to whom she had been forced to submit, she who had always feared to escape from infamy to death. Ever since Herman Front-de-Bœuf had murdered her father and butchered her brothers, she had been a drudge serving meat at his evening meals, and serving as meat for his nighttime meals (and his son Reginald's), or else for his special guests. Now this guest, one she had in tender teens invited to her castle, was upon her—his very clothing smelt unearthly. She tensed.

But his way was not the way of a man, for no man was he. He was vampire, and he was after blood, at least to begin with. Unbeknown to her, he had long intended to return to give to she who had died within, life—life intolerable, life inexhaustible, life inescapable. This night he had returned for just this purpose, being fêted by De Bœuf, to whom he had handed the castle on a platter.

He was annoyed to discover that Ulrica had not been treated as a maiden ought, in blatant disregard of the deal he had made, but what should he have expected, knowing that men are deceivers? He knew that at least his dishonourable host would offer her to him, and one should not offend one's host, even a fool. And Front-de-Bœuf was a born fool, belonging to a race of fools. Faugh, at times even being bound to a humanoid body disgusted Wulfgar, but that was a bondage he himself had accepted in a forgotten aeon before the dawn of man.

He had to make the best of it, even as the poor little vermin had to. For stern judgement awaited vampires who surrendered their bodies of flesh, a judgement best deferred. To tell the truth, he had a staggering and shameful secret long buried within his soul: his guests knew it, so did Usen. Though buried deep, it still haunted him. It was also an extra reason to stick with diaboloi and to stay away from Usen. His people did not know and must never know, lest they slay him.

Yes, his fear had to do with judgement. But begone morbid thoughts, her blood was refreshing, but enough was as good as a feast. And he who had taken was he who now gave. His fangs still within her neck, he secreted the cells of his own *élan vital*, a horizontal gene transfer of the life force that flowed through his veins, a DNA infused with his will. Henceforth she would live a doubly bound slave. A slave of her

Norman born overlords, now also a slave of one born before the world began, a morbidly unhappy creature bound to the orb of Tellus.

Henceforth her eyes and ears would be his, his pigeon, his informant within the castle, garnering news that fell from the rich man's table. For Ulrica still retained somewhat of her youthful beauty, and would still wait at tables when the Norman lords spoke freely as slaves to wine, and after table talk sometimes even more freely as slaves to the pillow. Henceforth he could see and hear what she did, and she would say and do whatever he commanded.

Hide it as he might, and hide it he did, he was not without pity, he who saw her pain. He who oppressed was also oppressed—a slave-host to diaboloi, to macrobes—and would allow her her vengeance in the sowing of mistrust and hatred between the new lords, the tyrant father and his savage son. And it would surely reap a harvest, for those murmurings would unerringly lead to murder on one of the many nights when divided father and son partook too deeply in an hour of drunken wassail. Then the slayer of her father would slay— or be slain by—his own son in unnatural hatred, hatred she would have cunningly sown. Then she would secretly smile as she saw the loser's blood flow and heard his dying groans—as he had heard hers. She who had died many times would partake of that blood, and refresh for a while her former beauty. Her body need never die while her master lived.

Ulrica felt the tickling of her blood. She was no stranger to death, she who had unhappily waited for her fate beyond the grave, she who had lived in unspeakable wretchedness. The Lady of Torquilstone, once alive and gay, had first died when her beloved father and brothers had been unjustly slain by Norman hands, hands that had then been laid secretly on her whom the world had believed slain with her kin.

That same night she had suffered her second death, as the ox-like face of her father's murderer had first breathed upon her fair face in lawless bands far removed from love. Love, she resentfully reflected, would sooner grace the regions of nether doom than Torquilstone's desecrated vaults in which she lived entombed. She now hated humanity. She who had been obeyed as an honoured Lady, had become scorned and insulted more than is woman's wont, but she would have her revenge. If only those hands and the son of those hands, hands that had caused her deaths, would die at her hands, then she would gloat and take some small comfort in that bitter irony. But for now she felt as if her mortal hours were numbered, for her head swirled in a swoon. Was it time to curse God and by his wrath die?

High time indeed, for she had become bitter of life, bitter towards the god who had betrayed her, though she had still sought to cling to his mother for womanly comfort. Her confused soul hovered between two religions, though in truth she knew little of either, little of how the Philikoi represented but roughly the Pantocrator in the old, and how the Pantocrator represented rightly himself in the new. But to her the new now seemed a cheat, a swindle: what on earth had been her sin, that the god of the cross had abandoned her soul to Helheim, to a life on earth of deep damning guilt? Why should the innocent suffer? And even if suffer they must, why so much more than the guilty?

Keep your thoughts pure? Refuse to do wrong? What a cheat! In half-heartedly turning her back on the old divinities—to such as Eostre, Hertha, Thunor, and Woden—she had made a bad deal. King Ethelbert of Kent had betrayed his country by the cross; bowing to the cross didn't pay; her rough image of the Theotokos afforded no protection. She should have wised up, cursed God, and sunken back into the cold comfort of paganism to escape her hauntings by day and by night. A fool she had been to have ever entertained the thoughts of blessing those who persecuted her—for so preached the cross—for how could she and why should she?

In the rising mist of death sing now the grim and glorious songs of bloody battles won, of outrageous fortune trodden underfoot. Hail Woden, we who are about to die sing of Rollo rather than of Richard. May the Seven Kingdoms be restored this day!

Then her own thoughts fled before the mist that was taking over her eyes. Time appeared to roll backwards and it seemed that out of body she floated within deep heaven, beholding a planet of liquid crystal, of moving colour and radiance ever weaving, a world of deep and profound beauty ever new. Warmth surrounded her ethereal body; sweet sharpness caressed her neck. Her hitherto world had withdrawn. Far above she saw first a vision of multitudes of spirits encircling this other world, darting into it as moths into a gaseous light, and soaring forth from it in unalloyed joy.

Then it seemed that happiness turned into horror, for after her trip returning reality showed her that now she was not her own but another's. It was undeath she suddenly sensed, corruption at a deeper level. She felt snared as a coney in a trap inescapable. She felt that the will of this man had become her will, a will enforced, an ill will to no human good. As if from blest drowning she resurfaced to bedevilled reality, still struggling to drown in bliss. She had died but yet lived. This man who wore no longer an angelic face, this man, she realised, was not a man, only a he. Long had her body not been hers; now even her soul was enslaved. Her body would live alone, and his will would live within. Poor Ulrica, was there no mercy?

By the dominance of a he not a man, she had died a third time, cut-off more deeply than ever from the light of life. By some mysterious prescience she saw that her days would be dimmer and her nights brighter—though of an eerie pale and sickly hue—and that her basic bodily appetites would transmute. Slops she would still stomach, but be needless to her stomach. Yes, her body would slowly drain of life, yet she would find that she could at will feign a face enough to encourage her tyrants to face her alone. And alone she would feed on them as they slept in their self-satisfied security, victims of their victim.

Just a little would those so drained wane, growing pale and spiritless. Just a little would she grow fat, rosy, and spirited. Few would notice the slight marks around their necks, though would feel curiously aged in the morning light, mortal life deservedly decimated. But Wulfgar would allow her no more blood than she needed to be a useful tool in his hands. Over slow years she must slowly appear more haggard just to keep up appearances. Then, fallen into seeming death, he would smuggle her body from the castle. Then he could awake her to be used elsewhere in his schemes. This she saw through his unholy eyes.

He returned to the feast in high spirits. The Norman sheep at the table assumed merely that a carnal fling had raised a smile, a not unheard of event in the history of the world—and they were all men of the world. But Baron Front-de-Bœuf had just cause to wonder about that smile. For it had come to his mind that he had never properly thanked Sir Wulfgar—by which title the stranger had introduced himself—for his judasical part in the storming of Torquilstone, and it suddenly troubled him to remember his flippant oath that Ulrica would indeed be left unmolested, an oath long honoured in the breach more than in the observance.

Still, that was water under the bridge, and Sir Wulfgar had raised no complaint so far. But now that he had sampled the goods, best let him sample some gold too: three things live on, girls, glory, and gold, but the greatest of these is gold. Front-de-Bœuf had ordered ten bags of gold to be brought into the hall to await his guest's return.

Sir Wulfgar had claimed to be from the north, and that Torquilstone had robbed his father's father in days gone by. Thus he had sold Front-de-Bœuf on the line that he was content for another to gain the castle, so long as Ulrica's family were slain and Ulrica was safe. Had he not flown off so soon, her safety from Norman lust might have been ensured. Why had he disappeared that night; why had he returned after these six years; what did he intend; and why did he smile? Front-de-Bœuf was wary: might Sir Wulfgar be planning on opening the postern gate to Saxon malcontents, a reverse betrayal? He quietly ordered his chief of guards to immediately triple lock that weak-point, for one who has bitten once might bite again. But with ingratiating smile he welcomed his unwelcome guest back to the feast.

"Sir Knight, I see that you have enjoyed our cellar wine, our fair little vintage of 1184. Though not the first to uncork that bottle, I trust that still it pleases your palate. Indeed you should have tasted first had you but stayed for our first night of revelry. But come, for your services bloodwine flowed freely—and that at your behest—and now pray be pleased with another token of my gratitude", and which point Front-de-Bœuf gestured towards the bags filled with rich gold.

"Gramercy," replied Wulfgar "for indeed the bloodwine you squeezed that night rejoiced the ghosts of my father and his father within the realm of Death's wife. As for the fruit of that vine, you were no doubt hard pressed to resist in my absence, but it is of little consequence. Indeed press now and drink your fill; let that that has been squeezed be squeezed again and again and feel the wrath of my house. As to these fresh tokens of friendship I gladly receive, and right willingly revive that friendship with my right hand, my lord."

It was better to allay than to alarm fears, and in fact Wulfgar intended no chastisement against the House of Front-de-Bœuf—what was done was done. The girl had suffered unduly, but so what? Far more to the point, the diaboloi had been appeased by the hecatomb of Torquilstone, so their hectoring had subsided. And he had at last made Ulrica his eyes and ears among the Norman nobles, and nothing but good could come of that. Also, his vanity was pleased to now see this hulk of a man sitting swellheaded before him but inwardly snivelling in fear. Vampires breathed in fear as breezes of sweet perfume. It was right that the vermin feared them.

As Lorell he was but a poor son of a hag, but he had many identities kept stealthily in local towns. Spared by Robin Hood he had in hostility entered Scafeld late that morning. For under other guise he held there house, horse, and helmet. Then as Sir Wulfgar he had ridden swiftly to Torquilstone. Earine was lost to him; Ulrica was lost by him: his mother need not know all.

Now he felt once more his mastery. He had been vexed by a pathetic little green man having checked him at Papilwik, but he had enslaved the friend of his enemy's friend, and that gave him a spiteful sense of satisfaction. But as he left Herman he felt only contempt for the pay-off in gold: whether ten bags of gold or thirty pieces of silver, he had never betrayed nor would betray even the baseborn for filthy lucre.

The mightiest of the vampires could happily pose as count or as commoner, and one as a dogsbody might be mightier than one as a duchess. As he left for Nottingham, he carried a letter worth more to him than a wagonload of gold. As for the gold weighing down his horse, crossing the Scheth he discreetly ditched it: gold had no hold on him. From the rising of the sun to the going down of the same, he road on through Moresburg, Stanleia, Belesovre, Tevreshalt, and Chirchebi. At last the castle of Nottingham was in sight, and soon he was ushered through into the presence of the sheriff.

"Hail my lord Sheriff, I come bearing Baron Herman Front-de-Bœuf's petition to command your men on a special operation to apprehend and hang the malefactor Robin Hood, once Earl of Huntingdon".

The sheriff readily read the document, but with little show of hope. "Sir Wulfgar, methinks you are not from these parts. Know you that this pernicious renegade has half the people aiding and abetting him, and the other half more than half afraid to speak ill against him, for he can be as ruthless as the next man. Thus we of Prince John have few friends and many enemies when seeking out this malapert. He is too cunning a fox to run to ground, to tree, or bring to bay, and has led my hounds many a merry chase, but still we follow when we have scent, and Sir Guy of Gisbourne not the least. Yet if we masters of the hunt have so far failed, will you Sir Knight fare better? For you know not the chase."

"Lord William, 'tis perhaps a case of setting a fox to catch a fox. For I have men, known only to me, who wander the forest of Shirewude in guise of outlaws. Should they be caught by foresters they must bite their tongues, for their families will die alongside them should they speak my name. Did you know that your foresters boasted of hanging Heaton of Bateleia? He had been one such spy, fearing me more than death. Some are with Robin Hood, and smuggle word out of Robin's whereabouts to vile merchant spies. Thus I can find the fox. All I lack are hounds to take the fox. For that I look to you in Baron Front-de-Bœuf's name, my lord."

In fact Wulfgar neither had nor needed a spy network, for he himself could easily spy out Robin's domain. Nor needed he soldiers for the kill, except that since the family of Marwolaeth walked softly under the watchful eye of Lilith, it was better to use humans to kill humans than to leave vampire footprints for those with eyes to see. Yet though a prudent plan, Wulfgar itched to have Robin at his mercy—at last he would reveal himself to Walleff's heir; at last he would have revenge.

Eleven   ᚤE OLDE FOX AND ROBIN

William de Wendeval was High Sheriff by the grace of the prince, and Herman was a favourite of the prince. It might be a wild goose chase ill justifying a commitment of many soldiers to Sir Wulfgar, but then the goose was worth yet another wild chase, even if plucked by another. It could not be helped. If he did not help Sir Wulfgar, he himself might be accused of protecting Robin Hood. And if Sir Wulfgar failed, why, his own failures would be in knightly company. So it was that Wulfgar got his soldiers, and that all they were told was that they must obey his orders without question. With that he led them off into the forest.

Very soon they discovered that their curious commander kept closely to the shade and slept outside of the camp at nights. For unbeknown to them, each night Wulfgar stowed his knightly garments securely in the trees beyond the perimeter watch, then in bat form swiftly searched sections of the forest for the Hood. In fact it did not take him long to discover that Robin's camp was for a while just north of Walesbi, and that Haughton Castle was covertly in league with the outlaws. With such a shield at his back and the Maun at his side, he no doubt felt secure to waylay travellers of the king's highway between Nottingham and York.

The next day Wulfgar rode with his chief guard to Haughton Castle, and there alluded to whispers that the castle turned a blind eye to breakers of the forest laws. "Of course," he added, "such baseless accusations are untrue, but all the more reason to be seen to help us now to purge the land of this band of rebel scum, proving beyond doubt your loyalty to the king." That veiled threat, along with the script from the sheriff and the attendance of his chief guard, was sufficient to cow the castle.

And so it was arranged that the castle would be the trap. To be that it had to implicitly admit that it had been a place where Robin would have felt safe within, but Sir Wulfgar promised that that implication would never be drawn against the castle, so long as it now played its part in Robin's capture. Kiss and make up.

The sheriff's men would divide and attack Robin's camp from the west and from the north. The outlaws would probably fight a bit, then when they felt they could lose the attackers, flee to the castle, for it afforded a strong hiding place for them: why would the sheriff's soldiers search a castle for outlaws? They could even disguise themselves as castle soldiers while any of the sheriff's men were delayed outside until they could prove right of entrance. A bit like when the Clerk of Copmanhurst had delayed entrance of his king to his hermitage, on grounds that a multitude of robbers and outlaws were abroad, or when the sheriff's men had been warned off from Arlingford Castle by Lord Fitz-Walter for, as he had said, in such uncertain times how was he to know whether they really were the sheriff's men and not outlaws trying to gain unlawful entrance? One must be careful! Castles could always delay unwelcome visitors, by hook or by crook.

Wulfgar could have singlehandedly dealt with Robin's night watch without much ado, but playing his part he was content to allow a dawn raid, allowing the outlaws enough light to see their chance of flight. If at all possible he wanted Robin kept alive for a slow and ignominious death. He'd like Robin to taste the horror of his men's torture and termination, too, so the more captured alive the merrier.

Yet unbeknown to Wulfgar, someone, like a silent hooded man, had espied him espying Robin, and had appeared to Robin as a vision in the night. "Hail Heir of Siward. I, Alessandro, bring you an heirloom far older than the seed of Siward. For here is a sword wrought before the dawn of man, yet gifted to your line for service beyond price. As befits your customs it was bestowed with the parents of Constance of York, through whom you are come, and I—since your line was cursed by the Dark Side—I became its keeper until such a time as this, for the point of need is now. Now be prepared, for an ancient warrior waits to attack at dawn. Yet now you have in hand Torodagnir, a weapon to your will, which no iron mace will shatter. Troll Bane it is called in your speech, for it was made in days when the race of trolls threatened the firstborn of Usen. It is a sword of a lesser spirit—some spirits resided so—and will do your will. Fear no evil, save the castle that has befriended you."

Little John saw only a sword piercing the rockface. If wielded by hand, that hand was unseen. With a cry he awoke the camp. Robin rubbed his eyes. The unknown visitor had simply vanished with the dream, as if he had never been. Yet there was his sword lodged deep within the rock. Instinctively Little John tried to withdraw the sword to hand to his master, yet the sword seemed at one with the rock. It was some minutes before Robin remembered a story long telling of a blade of Logres that had been similarly sheathed in a rock, which had only come out for he for whom it was intended, a symbiosis between man and sword, two spirits as one. With that in mind he took the hilt and easily withdrew the sword as if from water. With it within his hand, he saw visions of ancient days, and divined a hidden will and a hidden flame within.

With weapon in hand and warning in mind, he roused the camp just before the crack of dawn, putting them on high alert, and warning all to avoid the castle until more was known. His plan was to head to Bernysdale and lay low for a while, but his plan was nipped in the bud. For promptly at dawn the camp was attacked. From the north, with a hullabaloo noisy soldiers attacked the perimeter guards. A number of outlaws sprung to their defence, arrow against arrow. The rest looked to cross the Maun, but arrows from the west showed a contingent of soldiers across the river.

Yet surprisingly the attackers seemed content to merely exchange fire, rather than meeting sword to sword. Normally the outlaws would have left a small group to briefly act as a rearguard defence, while the main party made swiftly to Haughton Castle, but now Robin feared taking that path. Yet had he not been told to fear no other evil? If west, north, and south, were fraught with danger, should they flee east to Marcham, or should they stand and fight? Torodagnir in hand, he grimly decided to stand and fight. His own men were all well trained with both bow and sword.

Wulfgar stood watching from the trees. His men did not advance, inviting the outlaws to retreat into the trap. The attrition rate was much higher for his men, as they were poorly trained in archery. Any fool could use a crossbow, but they had their drawbacks. For starters, shooting time was much longer. If you shot, hid, and reloaded, your target might well have moved and be ready to target you when you reappeared. If you simply shot, stood, and reloaded, a half dozen longbow arrows could head your way before you fired again, and each longbow arrow was heavier so more deadly and accurate over distance.

A few soldiers had been dressed in Lincoln greens, armed with longbows, and positioned south of the camp. They lacked longbow skills, but their task was simply to beckon the outlaws to flee south into the castle—they were decoys. But Robin had ordered no retreat, so these soldiers failed to tempt his men to flee.

Changing tack, Wulfgar sent his surviving soldiers storming into the outlaws. Their numbers were higher—not all of Robin's men had been in the camp—but running from their shelter into the arrows of skilled longbowmen was the death warrant for many. Wulfgar himself feared not the darts of his puny enemy, kitted as he was with helm and mail shirt, with a curved kite-shaped shield that covered his body on the left. He wielded an axe, having sword girt at his side—a formidable sight to fling fear against his enemies. He enjoyed quicker reactions than humans, as well as greater resilience to attack, and in his pride he considered himself invulnerable. But he was not.

His men fell like ninepins before the volleys from Robin's men, but in turn they fell like ninepins before his axe. However, Robin was not the one to let others fight his battles. Dispatching a few soldiers with unusual ease, he realised that the knight behind the attack far outclassed his men. So it was that Robin focused on this champion, who met him in joyous combat.

The mighty axe descended on Torodagnir, only to find that it had met its match. For Torodagnir sheared through it like a hot knife through butter. Wulfgar instantly drew his sword and reinforced both Norman sword and shield by his own will, matching the will of Torodagnir. What he lacked was swordplay—never having needed to hone his skill to achieve victory in battle—and found that Robin's sword was getting through his defences.

Incredibly he was losing the battle to swordsmanship and sword, for the will of Robin's sword was greater than the added resilience which he gave to his own sword and armour. Meanwhile Robin's men, left only to fight human soldiers, soon had the upper hand. Soon the sheriff's men had been slain or had surrendered, many wounded by sword and staff. Robin signalled that he be left to fight alone this warrior, and soon had disarmed him of shield, and soon after of sword.

Wulfgar expected no quarter. His strength was well nigh drained away. With the severing of the green cord from around his right arm, his reserve power had been slashed away. In the rage of defeat the cowardice of flight was far from his mind—in short, his mind was in confusion. And now the point of Robin's sword was at his breast. "Yield, Sir Knight, and confess yourself defeated", shouted Robin. And Wulfgar stood stock still in amazement.

What man was this, who again showed him mercy? He removed his helm, and in turn Robin was amazed, for he saw before him none other than Lorell, son—or grandson—of Mother Maudlin the witch. But how could a ragged young man of the forest, cast out from a hovel one day, return the next in full knightly armour of Norman and Numinous make, commanding the sheriff's men? "Sir Lorell, I presume? Pray tell, why should I spare you this time who sought the life of Earine the last? Did I not warn against being found again in Shirewude? Speak sirrah!"

"That you still harbour mercy troubles me sore, and I would speak with you alone, for what I have to tell will endanger the life of any who hear it. Are you willing?" asked Wulfgar-Lorell. Robin stoked his beard and nodded dubiously, and indicating the cave followed with point of sword to back. Meanwhile his men tied up those of the sheriff's men who were able to fight or flee, and tended to those who were unable, both of their own and of the sheriff's. For Robin had always made clear that even those fighting for the sheriff were fellow human beings in God's likeness, and that good men could in ignorance and need fight for evil masters. Only when they were unable to be overheard did Wulfgar begin.

"Know you first that I am not as men, for I am not of the race of man."

"What, are you of Lilith, Adam's first wife", spluttered Robin. For since the episode with Mother Maudlin he had been pondering the tales of shapeshifters, morphs, and how the mother of all had stalked about as a spotted leopard, one whose name was Lilith, one who had married Adam before Eve—or so the tale went. Some had said that a warrior race had sprung forth from her loins, and here was a warrior indeed.

"Nay, Adam had but one wife, though the name you raise is feared by my people. But behold, my people preceded your people, and for the most part prey upon them as wolves upon sheep, though in clothing as sheep. What I say to you, noise not abroad, lest my life be forfeit by her whom you have named. Yet I am torn by death: tormented in life I would die, yet greater do I fear the torment to follow, for I am of the Kingdom of Night, the vampire kind. No child of Usen foresees the sure damnation that awaits us of unforgiveable sin. Yet to stave off that day I am doubly self-damned, for in millennia past I welcomed the diaboloi so as to stave off my death, and now their words within my head are an evil to me inescapable. For the most part I am the master; they the griping pain. So it is that I live a malingering death—but to die is far worse.

"Your forefather slew my brother Grindan, a death that enraged us who were in his immediate family. And yet we are under sovereign law not to reveal ourselves—a law I break to you now, for I am in double debt to your mercy, mercy that I crave not yet proves me craven. That law prohibits our revenge, yet revenge we must take, so are torn by that law, we who show no mercy. Your line has been cursed by us, even down to the shredding of your heart. Yet in that my mother—whom you call Mother Maudlin—to my bitter annoyance did but bungle. Therefore unbeknown to her and to my sister, I departed only to return in this guise—for I have several—to wreak on you my revenge. What? Did I love my brother so much? Master Hood, you understand me not. What has nothing to do with love has much to do with pride. For Grindan was in our pack, and a pack that loses its members to your kind, wears shame like a crown.

"Now comes your moment of decision. Twice you have shown me wretched mercy. Yet if what I detest I owe my life to, am I right to so detest? Now you know me for what I am, vampire, a leech unto death. Yet are there not animals you spare among you which slay you, that we alone should be slain on sight? If yet you spare me, my feud with the line of Walleff will have ended, and thus will I urge mother and sister: though know now that Marian can never bear children—but this was my mother's contrivance as she fled from Shirewude, and cannot be healed."

Robin stood in reflection. Incredibly the tale held together. The shadowminder of the sword had shown him that there was more to heaven and earth than his philosophy, as had his new sword. Maybe the creature before him was an imagodei, as he: he could not be sure although its fear of punishment after death pointed in that direction, and it was good to think that such evil would receive its due reward.

Yet if evil ought to be rewarded, ought he not reward it now by swift death? And if mercy said no, must mercy reward it by eternal death even if it could repent?

Though unhappily touched, touched it was by mercy, so it seemed capable of redemption. Yet however capable, it remained unredeemed and deadly dangerous. Yet seemingly in his debt, just as it had been when previously shown mercy. Fooled me once, fooled me; fool me twice, fool me. And yet.... "You said that knowing your identity meant death to the hearer. Would you kill, or have killed, me who now knows, even if your feud is ended? If I spare you as I might a wolf that merely feeds on man as its natural prey—as I have spared wolves—is there not a fate worse than death, that your kind inflicts on us? I have heard stories that that is so, superstition until this day. Do you not damn human souls to perdition?"

"We do not nor can we damn any soul but our own. While the enslaved live they live as undead, but true death severs the tie: their true heart, whether conceived towards or away from him, is always known to Usen the Judge—or so we have heard tell. But now I swear never to force enslavement on another, and to resist unto blood my guests. As to your knowledge, if it is traced to me my life will be justly forfeit, as will yours if traced to you. Yet it is for you to use within your heart. Write it down if you will, though mayhap as but fantasy, and bury it deep so that it will not be unearthed in the time of your mortal life. I will thus be content, for such a tale is unlike to be believed once you cannot vouchsafe it, and thus our lives will not be endangered. If you confirm your mercy, I shall soon go forth into isolation and solitude, to ponder the strange quality of mercy, an attribute of Usen himself. To learn from it, who can tell?"

"Then go!" said Robin, "And may I not repent my mercy." Not long ago Robin had shown mercy to Worman, who had turned from being servant to him to being seneschal of the sheriff. Worman, far from learning mercy, had since shown no mercy to the helpless, hanging them haplessly, and Robin had had him hanged—and high time too. Sometimes mercy was wasted.

Wulfgar bowed low. "My master, one thing more. If ever I have child, it shall bear your name in some small atonement for what my mother has deprived you and your lady of." Bitter words of comfort! There was some murmuring in the camp as the captured knight was brought out and released into the wild. His horse and gear he forsook, along with all further claim on the sheriff's men. They for their part were well cared for, and when all were sufficiently rested directed to the castle, for, said Robin, its loyalty to the prince was well known to all and it would without doubt welcome them.

Thus it was that Robin bestowed his blessing on the castle that had done him only good in the past, securing its safety for the immediate future. Yet long would it be before he could dwell close by again, he thought, for he guessed that the sheriff's suspicions would be raised against it, and guessed that men of the sheriff would for a while be ensconced as spies within its walls.

Wulfgar returned home to his Lorell identity, and to Marwolaeth and Kendra. His restless mind he would conceal from them; he must conceal from them. His enslavement of Ulrica would be enough to tell, and she of rich picking could serve them well as a family slave. Perhaps he should even have child by her, in some small token of his debt to mercy, but not now—in her next life, perhaps. But Mother would need some convincing after Grindan's foolish antics—no need to rush into such hasty marriage anyway, for she had perpetual youth and wasn't going anywhere.

Twelve   RELEASE FROM DEATH

When Wulfgar abandoned Ulrica to her room, six rotten years had just gotten worse. Where was love? She could now hear voices inside her head. Voices of raucous laughter as if coming from the banquet hall, to which Wulfgar had returned. Voices impossibly beyond being heard in her turret, and the scornful laugh of Kendra the gypsy woman repeating as a bad meal. Was she at last going mad? Please God no. In fear she forced herself onto her knees, clasping her hands and bowing her once proud head. "God, why is my life so hard? Why do I suffer so? Why have you made my days drag on, my nights miserable? If I beg you for nights to end, you lengthen them as I toss and turn until dawn, or sleep in inescapable torture—dreams and visions hold terror; choking seems better than waking.

"Towards hopeless trouble my life drains swiftly away. Then you won't see me, and like a body buried and a cloud emptied, I'll be forgotten. Unfair my fate and full of woe, a monster in a cage. Won't you let my meaningless life end? From sunrise to sunset, why bother me, look at me, stare at me? Can I not I even swallow unseen? Why target me with your bow? Am I so bad? Let me off and let me be, to die and trouble you no more." This god who had claimed to be God, had seemed happy to have made demands on her lifestyle when the sun was shining, but in her storm seemed happier to stay sheltered inside, looking out but not helping out, not even bothering to speak. So to his sin of standing back he added the sin of discourtesy! She was forlorn and forsaken!

Four more lonely years rolled by, in which her only gratification was the murder of Herman Front-de-Bœuf by his son, a murder she had inspired and covered up. Ulrica now had an appetite and power unseen. The plan was to soon remove her from the castle as if a corpse, allowing her to awaken elsewhere for future use, but the plan miscalculated her inner pain, and her inner strength of will. Suppressed for the time being, still her pain and will lingered on. Normans came and Normans went, and secrets spoken securely in Ulrica's hearing—secrets as safe as the grave, since she surely had no way of leaking intel. Thus her keeper had heard Norman rumours about local vampires. *Praemonitus, praemunitus*: forewarned, forearmed; burnt fingers dread the fire: vampires forewarned can escape from being burnt. When vampire hunters investigated the rumours they found no evidence of infestation—the enslavement of Ulrica had paid dividends.

But life dragged on. One day changed all that. For one day the castle came alive with braggadocio, for a cavalcade from the Gentle and Joyous Passage of Arms of Ashby—otherwise known as the Royal Carnage of Ashby de la Zouch—Saxon nobles unprotected by Prince John, had been captured in the greenwoods by masked assailants, who had proved to be of Torquilstone.

For Maurice De Bracy, impatient to marry into lands of a Saxon heiress, fearing King Richard's unexpected return, and advocating a total subjugation of the Saxons, had conspired with the Templar Brian de Bois-Guilbert, to together disguised as outlaws, capture the Saxon band. At first they planned to later doff their outlaw disguises and in their own persona feign a rescue and force the Saxon princess' hand in holy wedlock.

With such in mind, the Lady Rowena, along with her father Cerdic and noble Athelstane of Coningsburgh, had been caught in a snare, together with two ethnic Jews—Isaac of York and Rebecca his daughter—and a bandaged, unidentified, invalid. Yet the conspirators had modified their plan, the one suddenly distrusting the other with his prize, and so taken in their own guise their prisoners into Torquilstone, using intimidation instead of trickery. There the baron had opened wide the gates in hospitality, and the three Norman knights had drunk to an ambush successfully achieved, and to rich pickings to come.

As fate would have it, their joy would soon be cut short. Reginald would realise that ethnic Jews were human after all, and burn in the hatred of that knowledge. Maurice would see his bird released and himself under the paw of the lion. Brian would flee with his bird, yet would die to release her, and their tales, as that of the invalid, would become well told by Sir Scott of Scotland. Now into their tale came Ulrica. She had met the Jewess Rebecca with scorn and contempt, unsympathetic to that young daughter of old Zion. Ironically it was Brian, an evil man of little conscience, who became so swayed by Rebecca's dignity that he would put her own interests before his, at least in hope of gaining her. Why, he was even prepared—against his most holy Order—to actually marry her, a Jewess, to his undying infamy, but she wouldn't have him, the ungrateful wench!

But it was a dignity that moved also Ulrica, reminding her of days of innocence and of life. And then had come a rescue attempt, when Wamba, fool of a jester, servant of Cerdic, had foregone freedom to offer his life in exchange for his master's. And then a rescue attempt when Cerdic had challenged Ulrica to seek a good death—that challenge had sunk in as deep as a knife. Cerdic had understood Ulrica as little as he had his son, seeing little her stresses and strains. He had left. His was to see to the storming of the castle alongside the mysterious Black Knight and the gallant men of Shirewude Forest. She who could not leave freely in life, had decided to leave freely by death.

Telepathically she heard her soulmaster speak: "Ulrica, I forbid your death. Stay and be freed. I shall come if needs be and overthrow this castle, but you I shall use elsewhere. You need never die."

Nevertheless Ulrica had determined that having betrayed her honour to save her life, that at last she would arise and overthrow the human tyrants that had so long enslaved her. "No, I shall not be their slave, nor yours any longer. This day the daughter of Torquil shall have both her revenge and her release. This day she shall burn."

"There is no need. Everlasting life is yours."

"No, there is need, and the life you give I would give for death."

"But is slavery not better than death? I too am a slave to my guests, as they are to their great master. Yet if freedom is death, is it not the door to eternal damnation? My kind are rebels to the Light. We fear judgement beyond death so fear the doorway of death. My own body is part kept by my guests, diaboloi I have invited to dine, diaboloi who have preserved my body. I bear this, and grant you too the gift of cheating death. What good awaits you after death, Ulrica, that you seek freedom from life? Why should I release you to your folly?" Wulfgar simply could not see it. She had chosen neither divinities nor Deo. Falling between both stools, what future had she with either? Neither would accept a foxhole convert who too late begged forgiveness for past ingratitude, one who had served the Night. Her best bet was to put off the evil day of reckoning. On the Dark Side she had power, and should endure insults of the flesh in order to drain her persecutors of their lifeblood one by one—to gain the last laugh. Why not live on hate, she who could not live on holiness?

"But master, what price do you yourself pay for your mortal life? I sense in you great bitterness in the Great Game. You are vampire; your guests are diaboloi. As you are gifted to see with my eyes, so you have gifted me to see with yours. I see times before my time, diaboloi incurably evil by nature, filling the whole world with tears, despair, and suffering, in hatred of Usen. I see he and she diaboloi[ii] causing wanton damage and wilful disruption, bringing confusion, disaster, illness, and mental troubles beyond reckoning. I see diaboloi attacking the moon, manifesting on Midgard their fury as dragons, hurricanes, desert storms—even as inescapable draughts within homes. I see them kept in check by Usen and his agents of power, not by human might. And I see that vampires are otherwise—though Lamaštu sides with the kingdom of her adoption. I see that vampires of the Night aim not to harm for harm's sake; that they delight in blood but not in death; that they hold man in disdain but not in hate; and that they are kept in check by human might, not by Usen and his agents of power. You are vampire; your guests are diaboloi. I see your own anguish against your slavery to evil will. I see you newly challenged by twice-given mercy. You, who would be freed, grant I pray you my freedom to pass beyond to my destiny, grant me mercy."

Wulfgar's heart was touched by her plea, and he admitted to himself the truth of her insight—he was unhappily bound for life. Only a millennium ago he had heard a moral imperative about treating others as you wished to be treated. Ever since Cuiviénen his heart had been touched with compassion for the people of Usen, and he had walked in delight with daughters of Eve though never with daughters of Iminyë. But his deeds were evil. And more so, perhaps, were those of his mother.

Would she forgive a son who released a valuable bird from its cage, a bird beyond recapture? For Ulrica had already proved her worth to his camp in warning them about Norman threats. And his own guests had used her to foment Norman trouble such as blood feuds among the noble families, all part of the Great Game they played so skilfully. Ulrica had a bright future as a *corrumpi*, and he would be punished for letting her go: but was he himself not let go a mere four years ago?

Yet adoption came with a baggage of both privileges and responsibilities, and to fail in the latter could invoke death. The humans had similar stories. He reflected on when Mardoqueu of Shushan had adopted his orphaned niece Edissa to be his daughter. In those days their blood enemies, the Amalequitas had sought mass destruction of their people, but the tables had been turned by Edissa's high risk adventure. It had involved putting her life on the line—all because of her adoption—and though a good girl she'd resented the responsibility, as did Wulfgar, son of Marwolaeth. He felt trapped like Edissa: "If I perish, I perish." Ulrica still had a beauty in her heart that moved him to risk his own neck, a beauty that Cerdic had awakened.

"I shall grant what you call mercy. Child, I shall break your chain and think of you no more. You shall be free to take your own course and to melt your shackles in your own fire. Do you thus return to the faith of the cross?"

"Nay," she replied, "I deem it too bitter; it has helped me not. My death shall be to Father Woden and Brother Vidar, a death of bitterness and sweet revenge. But I thank thee for my freedom at last, and wish thee well. Farewell!" She who had dabbled in the new thus returned to the old, unaware that the old was of the new, unaware that love awaited beyond her doom. Bitter-sweet indeed was her doom, she who had rejected the looming and shrouded monk's warning, and by not escaping Torquilstone had sealed its fate. She remembered how the spectre had warned her that unless its warning was heeded her head would be raised in flames—let it be so, and so it was.

How fared her friend Marian, she wondered. For her part she had told Cerdic to await her sign, the sign both of Rahab's salvation and of Ulrica's doom: victory through death seemed possible now that she was yielded to death as to a husband. For Cerdic had joined the besiegers, telling them to engage the enemy, and to press the attack once they saw a red flag waved from the eastern turret. For Ulrica had first descended to where was stored a stockpile of fuel below where now lay dying the wounded Reginald Front-de-Bœuf, and set it ablaze. Her body would along with that parricide be consumed body and bones. She hastened to his bed, thus to torment him who had oft tormented her, then leaving him helpless ascended the turret to wave the red flag, for by then pressing their fight, the Saxon army would prevent the defenders from fighting the fire.

At that sight Robin of Shirewude sprang forward with his archers, as the defenders threatened to bury the Black Knight and Cerdic the Saxon under a stone pinnacle of the battlements above the postern gate. It was only then that too late the defenders discovered the peril of fire. In the courage of despair they sought the safer defence of the barbican, yet there were soon defeated. The dying laughter of Ulrica rang loud throughout the castle, her laughter of freedom giving no comfort to the dying man: the last laugh was hers.

Thirteen   The Judgement Seat of Lilith

How came Marwolaeth ever to live in Papilwik? Were the machinations of the moirai behind the meddlings of the vampires? Could matters have been otherwise? Long had the smoke of Grindan's body been lost to the four winds, as water under the bridge. And the smoke of Torquilstone remained in the unfixed future. Since vampire vengeance against the secondborn was a noble luxury they could ill afford, it was strictly forbidden: personal vendettas jeopardised the existence of the Night. Yet in defiance of the law, the House of Marwolaeth had sought its private revenge against the House of Walleff.

The problem had not immediately come to light, but Marwolaeth's house had previously been flagged up as an unruly one, more prone to bite the hand that struck one cheek, than to turn the other. Yes, in an ideal world you would bite off that hand and spit it out, but alas the world was not ideal. Vampires had to play by the rules, keep under cover, and not reveal themselves. To preserve identity was to preserve life. Too many stories had already circulated since the lazy hazy crazy days of Sumer.

Thus it was that Lilith regularly had had her children circulate, proactively gathering reports of possible breaches of the rules. Draven it was who, doing the rounds, had picked up on Grindan's death. Knowing Marwolaeth's disposition, he had investigated.

Clearly Walleff had been responsible for Grindan's lawful death— fine, play with fire and get burnt. Clearly Grindan had been a fool but a lawful fool—enslavement was a permitted but precarious pastime. Clearly Walleff's fortune, and that of his house, had soon suffered deeply—so what, humans were a miserable bunch. Walleff had lost his first wife, had been betrayed to death by his second wife, had had his heir removed from the inheritance by his second wife, the second wife had flown from her uncle's wrath, and her daughter had in the year of their lord 1111, divided the inheritance between two husbands. Plenty of spills and thrills, but was there a culpable connection with Marwolaeth's house?

Draven had questioned some who had known Walleff, who told of a birth party spoilt by a mysterious prophetess, who had foretold vengeance for the death of Grindan. Draven had found that disturbing, feeling it all too likely that he could put a name to that prophetess within two guesses. It was just the kind of thing which Marwolaeth or Kendra would do, crowing their curse to enrich the pain. Would his people never learn the wisdom of Lilith in forbidding vengeance, of not making rods for their own backs? Vampire meddling wasn't clear cut concerning Walleff's first wife, yet his second wife had justified her betrayal of her husband by telling of his infidelity, he who had not sinned against her.

Who were the accusers who had visited Judith? Again he had thought that within three guesses he could name both. A betrayal was foretold. Since vampires could not predict the future it was up to them to make good their declaration of intent. It would fit the pattern that they had personally wound up Judith to work their will. Draven had continued to probe each outcome of the curse, perceiving the hand of the House of Marwolaeth.

And thus he had reported back to Lilith his queen. And thus Lilith had summoned them, and doomed that the House of Marwolaeth be confined for a time to Papilwik, a small out of the way of trouble place, within that tiny out of the way of history island. They were to cool their heels there for a while, and purge their hearts of revenge. Their rehabilitation would make life easier for everyone. Though humiliation is hard to forget, they had to get over it and stop endangering the kingdom—kingdom safety was more important than any individual or household. And thus had matters stood between the queen and this house under her disfavour. As time moved on, Lilith noticed that the human houses of Matilda oscillated between the houses of Simon and of Dauíd. But that seemed pleasantly human politics, nothing to imply vampire intervention. She hoped that the House of Marwolaeth was respecting her judgement, and keeping its nose clean from any more back biting.

Confined by royal decree to Papilwik, human history was moving on undisturbed. The fury of Marwolaeth-Maudlin had died down to an ember. Inexplicably Lilith herself then began to meddle, not practicing what she preached. OK, she felt that her kingdom had been unjust to the House of Walleff. Of course it had, but she had no right to feel it, and still less to make amends. Hands off! If a problem dies away, bury it, and don't dig up the departed, the bitterness long subsided. Between you and me, one had to question the queen's fitness to rule.

Then the moirai stirred once more, mischievous fates playing their games, moving pawns and princes around. The Heir of Walleff arose in the Greenwoods, under the very noses of the House of Marwolaeth. Marwolaeth had been forbidden from fulfilling her prophecy against the House of Walleff. Fine, she had been slowly coming to terms with that, satisfied that at least substantial irreversible damage had been done.

But what had Queen Lilith decided to go and do, except to reignite that rage by reversing the irreversible? She had told Ishtar to look into the banishment of Egbert, and Ishtar had discovered the testimonials of Walleff's innocence, in particular Judith's remorseful recantation of the false testimony that had led to Walleff's execution and to the disinheritance of Egbert. Judith had lamented both her overly hasty and overly trusting reaction to a simply suspicious accusation. So what? Let sleeping dogs lie; let injustice long buried rot peacefully in the sodden sod. To right yesteryear's wrongs is to unearth a can of worms.

But no, having boned up on local politics, Lilith saw an opportunity with the coronation of Prince Richard, to have the testimonials handed to him. And Robert, Shirewude born and bred, safely unnoticed under the very nose of Marwolaeth, had been taken to Huntington by Richard. But the minute Richard had turned his back on his country—to play a friendly war game or two with Saladin—Robert had fled home in fear of Prince John, fled right into the arms of Marwolaeth. A right carry on. With his identity in the public domain, it was really only a matter of time before the House of Marwolaeth wrapped him within its web of vengeance, ultimately to his death. No, not ultimately, but that is another story. But how fared Wulfgar-Lorell, who having been spared by Robin, had spared Ulrica?

Well Wulfgar, as has been told, was upset by mercy, a strange concept, and even stranger to him to learn lessons from the Children of Usen. Being spared once by Robin, it was fully justified to slay

Robin another time. If a fool lets you strike again, strike harder! Repeated mercy should have been no more than more water off a duck's back, yet somehow Wulfgar allowed mercy to ruffle his feathers and to get under his skin. Far worse, he himself showed mercy, setting free a useful slave. His mother and sister couldn't help but know that, for though he had been her direct handler, she had been the family slave. He had known the risk but had hoped that they would let it pass, at least if he soon provided a replacement slave, someone happy with bondage. However when he returned home that time, he really wished he hadn't.

Weeks passed. Under Nindara, any vampire that sided with Usen's children, except for advantage, was to be cut off—by death from the body. Any family members of any such rebel were to be cut off—by death from the kingdom. No vampire was permitted to execute another without permission from the courts, unless as a matter of self defence. Wulfgar, returning empty handed—but intending to seek a willing family slave—still hoped that the family would draw together to hide their shame, hoped to ride it out: shame me; shame yourself!

He had underestimated mother. Marwolaeth would gladly have slain her surviving son, claiming self defence, but he might prove too strong. She might be slain by him if she fought alone—why put her own life at stake by a high risk strategy? Kendra might help; Kendra should help, but sister might fight for brother, and anyway Kendra would become accessory to the crime, and if suspicions were raised, could seek leniency by betraying Marwolaeth as instigator. Ideally Wulfgar would die and only Marwolaeth would know why, but if that wasn't going to happen, then what? Should he get away with it, so that none should know of her shame, or should she report him to the relevant authorities, exposing her shame at having such a wayward son? One son had been a fool; one son had become a knave. "Kendra, what should become of Wulfgar? His crime remains unpunished."

"Mother, I am of two minds. He has both given to us and taken away; enslaved and released. Should his name be praised or cursed? In the giving he showed no mercy to the human creature, but in the taking away he showed mercy to her but not to himself. That is an attitude celestial, and not to be forgiven. But isn't it prudent to overlook it? Who knows of it besides us? Besides, our people diminish and Wulfgar is strong, a very present help in times of trouble. Why not bury our shame if none else know of it? Might we not say merely that his guests impelled him to sacrifice her on their altar, and thus explain away her death? Why must the truth come out, when the truth will cast us out?"

"Daughter, my bitterness is raging and my rage is deep. Days I cannot sleep for troubled mind. Besides, if ever it came out, would we be spared from death by our silence? And it might come out. He has shown before a softness to women of that accursed race, though never before at cost to himself. What if he again commits selflessness? Is he rebelling towards the Light? Such treachery must be put down with a strong hand. Would you be willing to be such a hand?" asked Marwolaeth.

"No indeed. He is stronger than I. If combined our strength would win but we would be diminished, yet if the courts discovered that we had taken the law into our own hands, then their hand would be heavy against us. Think how Grindan's death was investigated. I would not risk their wrath, even to avoid yours." Kendra had wondered before whether adoption into a different family wouldn't have been wiser, or even adopting one of her own. Still, that was too late now. She had earnestly hoped that mother would let this scandal drop: obviously that hope wasn't going to fly. So sadly the truth would probably have to come out, unless they could trick Wulfgar into a fatal trap, such as had fooled Nindara a while back.

But Wulfgar was neither dotard nor dense, and he would be on the alert against any such trickery: those forewarned are forearmed. If mother could but wait a millennium or so, catch him off guard. But no, her impatience and her fears were obvious, and she was not one to be patient over patent wrongs.

So, since it seemed that Wulfgar had to be punished, and that they could not punish him privately, it only remained to get the courts involved, and presumably the sooner rather than the later. Already there would be questions as to why notification had been delayed, though all would know the answers: how sharper than a serpent's tooth is a thankless child! Marwolaeth's child, so privileged, had so thanklessly betrayed her trust, for which he must die and his family must be permanently expelled.

Thus her rage risen well above her safety, Marwolaeth contacted senior vampires of her island corner, who would convene a local court to hear the evidence and pronounce a verdict. The vampire court was soon assembled, six parents of six local camps, both mothers and fathers. But before dealing with Wulfgar, she and her daughter had had to make confession. Then that out of the way, Wulfgar had been summoned. "Wulfgar, how do you plead?" asked the convener, Deorc.

"I plead guilty, and as such have a right to unimpeded statement", replied Wulfgar. "Hear me well, my judges. My history and my power you know well. I, being true to the Night, had supplied many a servant. In so doing I have imparted strength to them by weakening myself, that our people would be served with useful information to their good. My slaves have lasted long and served well, yet have all gone the way of flesh, returning in death their power to me.

"It is true that I have walked with some few slave-brides of my choosing, which is neither harm nor help to our people and is permitted under our law. I have been blameless until this day, indeed my Darkness darkened once I opened myself to the Turannoi for my protection. Again, many of us have such pacts—it is not against our law or our custom. Yet over millennia uncountable our cooperation has never endangered our Kingdom of Night by diabolical death fury, and I have too held back their full malice against man, that malice not shared by vampires. This our queen knows well and commends: I have her favour, I who was once the vampire chief of this land, until my joining.

"Hand in glove with diaboloi, many a human tribe has waged war through my machinations, and never has court sat in judgement for crimes towards the Dark. Why now for crime towards the Light? Against Quintus Petillius Cerialis, at Wincobank I once took a spear to the heart, ending my days but for my guests, yet well I knew that their help was for their tool, even for the weakened tool I had become. Then they did bind me closer than ever, and you have no power to deliver me except unto death. Yet smugly superior you would not share my fate, and disdain the diaboloi for their total Darkness.

"I have looked deeper into their pit, into which we all slowly slide unwittingly. See you not that your hearts are as theirs, though still of lesser degree? Is there no protection from their subversion by letting in a little Light? Why must you condemn any move away from their Darkness? Yet no heretic am I. I do not bow before Usen the Light, I who have taken life from the Dawn. But, I ask, why blame his children for his sin of shackling us to this planet of frustration? Do they not share our shackles? Are they too not prey for diaboloi, at times hosting them even as do we? Have they and we not some commonality of Dark enemy, that at whiles we may not show them some mercy—perhaps receive some?"

"Enough," screamed Deorc, "He has blasphemed! What further need do we have of witnesses? Behold, you have just now heard the blasphemy. He has likened us, we who hate not man, with diaboloi who hate man. Humans are our food, which we hate not, but it is our law that we show them no mercy, nor seek any. His brother, had he lived, would have been flogged ragged for begging for it. We stand where we are, between the Kingdom of Necros and the Kingdom of Dawn, as the Kingdom of Night, turning not to either. He confesses that he showed that woman mercy, and suggests that we learn from the Light. Bah, away with such a one from the face of the earth; for it is not fit that he should live."

The other judges stopped their inner ears, for they could hear, or not hear, according to telepathy among their own kind. Deorc was the senior judge. At his insistence they adjudged that enough had been said, and cut their votes in revered tradition. Six bleeding right arms signified unanimity for Deorc's pronouncement. Wulfgar's action, and more so his radicalism, endangered their kingdom. Death from the earth take him, and death from the kingdom take his family, who had allowed him such opinions.

"I am standing before the judgement-seat of the queen, by her judgement I should be judged. I appeal to my queen", shouted Wulfgar. Much as they yearned to crucify him, they held back, knowing that refusing his appeal to the queen could bring her reproach down on their heads—she could neither legally nor safely be ignored, and Wulfgar had had her favour. To the queen he had appealed; to the queen he would go. It was little doubted but that she would affirm their judgement; payment was only put off. As was the custom, the judges escorted the prisoner to the royal residence.

And so it was that night that Lilith sat on the seat of judgement, and heard both prosecution and defence. As queen, it was hers to uphold the law. Yet as reigning monarch it was also hers to modify if needed the law of previous monarchs. However, vampire monarchs were not tyrants, and had to operate within bounds of acceptability. The Great Council had made her, and it could break her—at the risk of civil war. If given the case, would it probably vote the same way as this local court? If so, prudence dictated that she go with the flow, condemning Wulfgar to oblivion and his family to ostracism. She herself had had inner doubts as to the common assumption that Usen's children should merely be treated as food. Was that not a biased and bitter reaction to their imprisonment to Thulcandra, this silent planet?

Most had no such doubts, and held her in high regard well deserved. Though unsuccessful, to her credit she had proved her deadly intent on Usen's Foretold. Of course to her debit she herself had married one of the firstborn (a tolerated sin) and even had child by him. Yet to her credit she had butchered her child shortly after its birth. Yet to her debit that butchery pained her still with a pain hidden to most— but less than a handful knew that shocking secret. Lilith was a popular monarch, acting wisely and with discretion. Should she rock the boat?

Lilith rose: "Wulfgar, by your mercy a slave was released at loss to us and at gain to her, and both are forbidden. Moreover this loss was at risk to you. Such weakness undermines our people. Now I must pronounce your doom.

"Under Nindara, you should be henceforth executed, and your family disavowed by our kingdom. Yet under Lilith, though humans must be seen as unfavoured food, occasional mercy—for a little toxin can produce an antitoxin—can be seen as honouring and reinforcing the un-hatred that we have—that distinctive we have—from the diaboloi. Moreover, you have erred at times beyond mercilessness, thus to err this once into mercy can balance somewhat the pull of hatred. And you have been true to yourself, for you know too well the inner pain of slavery to the Darker side. Some vampires understand.

"Nonetheless penalty is prescribed, lest the creeping 'occasional' become the overwhelming 'common'. Penalty under the old law shall be commuted, to thy family and to thee. You are banished from kith and from kin, from camp and from kingdom, doomed to walk alone save with your guests without whom you would soon die, but with whom you are so tormented. Nor shall you partake again of slave-bride while I remain as queen. And you shall go forth flogged by the court. Your family under the old law should be banished from the kingdom. Yet, though it divined not your mind and delayed its duty to the court, its sentence too shall be reduced.

"For two hundred suns its freedom of flight shall be clipped, and it shall live in its forest, vulnerable to hob, man, and sindeldi. If it bypass these barriers, it shall be punitively punished by the court. If it is threatened, no help shall the kingdom give; if it is slain, no vengeance shall the kingdom take, for it shall abide in disgrace, until mayhap it effaces its affront." She sat down.

Those for the prosecution were affronted, but to up the ante was to invite civil war, for many would fight to retain Lilith as queen, and many would fight to dethrone her as queen. Might the Great Council itself divide? After all, the sinners were going to be punished; the damage was being contained. Their demands were being met by a heavy hand, howbeit not a deadly hand. It was true that tradition allowed previous law to be modified. To dispute that could endanger their own lives before the Great Council.

But Marwolaeth was enraged. In her books his punishment was far too lenient, even though in line with his, hers had been reduced—to smooth her ruffled feathers? Kendra was pleased to take her punishment and begin a new chapter—clipped wings and confinement for a few more years and good riddance of an unwanted brother—like a mere smack on the hand with a teacher's ruler. Wulfgar bowed his head, accepting the queen's decree of a life sentence. A flogging was no trifle, and the court would take out its anger on his body and will.

Following the rules, as a bat he took flight, and immediately Deorc and his fellow judges pursued. Bolts of thelodynamic power searing from their hand-wings into his body, the power of their wills in deep amaranth, byzantine, crimson, maroon, red, and scarlet. With each bolt his body shook, as he was battered but not broken. Of necessity his guests reinforced his will, keeping body and soul together, sharing somewhat his pain: to lose their slave was to lose their home, and if they lost that then they might as well go to the pigs.

As an enveloping cloud of darkness, together they fled, until the fury of the pursuers had been spent. Long had they pursued; long had his body been battered and scarred. Exhaustively he sought refuge in a broken down house in Lid of the North Ridings, just a little south of Witebi, there to recover. It had been a flogging and a half, and without citizenship he remained prone to any Dark vampire he encountered, to be beaten up at will. News of his banishment would be telepathically circulated, and it was wisest to lie doggo for a century or two, change his name, reshape his humanoid appearance, muddy his history.

As for Lilith, she knew that the case would win her no plaudits. The accusers of Wulfgar had gone, following his wake. Her family attended her alone, Ishtar and Draven, insiders of her inner secrets, yet puzzlingly loyal confidants. If she went down, family would go down, and they knew it. But the local court had not appealed her judgement, and so so far she and her subjects were safe.

The months moved on. She must not show any outward signs of uncertainty, of self-doubt, but self-doubt she secretly had. Nindara's law had been clear and popular: you knew where you stood, any infraction and the chopper came down. Humans were not to be hated, of course, but the Light was, and mercy was of the Light. Strange, come to think of it, that while claiming neutrality the Dark was never to be hated—did that show bias, the enemy of neutrality?

Now she herself had shown mercy, though she had tried to hide it under guise of his eventual restoration to the kingdom for the kingdom. She had once fostered ideas that Usen's children had some inner dignity and ought to be respected, and she could empathise somewhat with Wulfgar. Nindara had bullied her out of speaking such thoughts. Wulfgar had gone the extra mile—a subversive idea that had recently plagued Rome.

For proud Rome had had a policy of threat and intimidation to compel vassals to haul army baggage for upto a mile, and was proud of being bully to the underdogs. The last thing a bully wants is for a victim to offer sincere friendship, inviting them onto the losing side. Therefore it was no wonder that they had been narked when among the subjugated peoples, some, acting as if slaves of one whom Rome had unjustly butchered, started to offer to haul luggage an extra mile—some strange policy of non-retaliation over personal abuse, of actually caring for those they should hate, voluntarily exceeding unjust obligations.

The Roman mind objected to what it could not understand, food becoming a friend. It was true that some of these slaves to the crucified taught that resistance was sometimes permitted, but they seemed to add that it was never permitted as hate, and seemed happy to absorb personal attack. How such nice people could come out of such a nasty world puzzled Lilith, and in the light of Wulfgar combined to make her rethink one or two things

Fourteen   *E*XCOGITATION

Marian's short years of bliss had slipped by all too quickly, and childless Robin had ridden out of her life. Some said that she had soon become another's bride, believing Robin to be dead to her. Had it been worth it? The House of Marwolaeth had been brought low by its interference with the House of Walleff. Lilith too had interfered, unintentionally making matters worse. Now her heart and wisdom were being seriously questioned, and for what? The Heir of Walleff was once more all but forgotten, all but a legend. Had it all been worth it?

Lilith sighed. "A plague on these days, my friends. Once our people were united and we were stronger. We have become weaker with the passing of the years, and disunited. And I remain shackled to my people."

"Mother, you maintain the good will of the Great Council, though it is true that some others complain about your heavy shepherding of your people", said Ishtar.

"Heavy shepherding for heavy sheep, my daughter, but it wearies me nonetheless. Our law of non-intervention must be strict, and even the queen must not be above the law: I must shepherd myself more carefully. But intervention to curse makes the humans more aware of us, and with that increases our danger. What if we defy the extremes of Light and of Dark, and risk their wrath? What if we reveal ourselves to the secondborn in war to enslave their race? Will not many of us die the sooner, by human hands? Would the Kingdom Powers and aggeloi really stand idly by? No, we must not intervene to harm by hard hand or by soft, and yet some of our number have blatantly revealed rather than concealed their presence.

"In Ultra Silvam, Count Dracula has so tried my patience that I have had to clip his wings. Would that he would hammer his sword into a plough! For the humans there have taken to all sorts of superstitious defences. Discovering his allergy to garlic, they have yet to discover that many vampires relish it. Though they are fools, they are fools now more aware of us. Even though I put the count under some curbs, such as only taking those who enter his gates with thanksgiving, I fear that soon he will grow rebellious as his fear of death grows apace. And in the Land of the Yellow River, Jiangshi's followers have again made waves—they should be but silent undercurrent. And here there is Marwolaeth: will she show restraint and in time seek my face, or rebel against our kingdom?"

"Troubling times indeed my mother," said Draven, "and unlikely to get better. For we fear to face Usen and are kept safe only by life, yet as we feel death approaching—be it in ten hundred thousand years or days— we seek ways to lengthen our days. You confine Count Dracula to live as a web based, not a hunting, spider, yet afore long he will surely come forth from his lair and hunt for longevity. The Jiangshis are quelled for now but doubtless will resurface throughout their land. Maybe Marwolaeth will comply, whether or not from a willing heart, with your judgement. But others too defy you. Though few, rebels multiply and are as yeast. Yet without your royal hand our people would suffer calamity. Your majesty's wisdom keeps us within safe boundaries."

"And yet Draven," replied Lilith, "Rangda has been whispering that my caution is to protect the secondborn! And that I intervened—a curse on my folly—to bless the Children of Usen! That grimalkin might need her claws clipping before much longer, for by spreading discontent she risks civil war. Do you both still stand with me, your minds free from doubt?"

"My queen, in the days of Sumer I chose between the two of you, and I do not repent my choice", avowed Draven. "However, Rangda would make a strong though incautious queen, and were you to step down I could, howbeit with reluctance and hope mingled, support her election. But I serve you gladly as best hope for our people. You are wise, and do not put yourself before your people. And your sorrows teach you."

"As for myself," said devoted Ishtar, "I have long been to you as friend. That friendship I shall not betray, come what may. I too see your selfless commitment to our somewhat selfish people, who would each do whatever seems right for their own personal profit if there were no monarch, bringing mayhem. Long may your wisdom guide thy people."

Lilith could see dedication in her children, yet still suffered from unease within. Without there were fightings, and within there were fears. Fear even that she was too mindful of humanity, not as a fisher is mindful of a fish, but as one imagodei is mindful of another. Yet she resisted Usen—had he not bound them by the Eighth Law? Yet why did some of her people side with him? Why did he side with the weak, the secondborn? Why had Hamashiach come, Usen's champion, who it was said, had dethroned death through death? Was her unconfessed love for her people, an unwanted child? Was she heading for disaster? She must entomb her doubts. She was queen of vampires. But Wulfgar had unintentionally planted seeds of doubt and of hope.

That night Lilith had set off immediately after dusk to see one of the secondborn, for reasons of a personal nature. That night she flew to Shirewude, for in that forest seeds of mercy had been sown in Wulfgar, once mighty among the vampires, seeds that spoke strangely to her heart. For her daily torment was of her own lost daughter, lost mercilessly. That ingrate—a term by which Lilith had justified her murder—had turned the better part of her affection towards her own miserable children, ignoring the fact that she remained the direct link that Lilith had had to her former husband, a link of affection that she still had somehow needed.

Needed affection? Vampires needed no affection. That need had been alien to her, yet had been within her. Well, maybe it made sense that humans were told to give no place to the devil, but it made no sense to tell vampires to give no place to affection: islands don't cry, but she cried, so was not an island. Why had she married, if not for affection—and companionship? She didn't like to admit it, but she had sought affection from a husband, then from a daughter. By a nephil she had lost the one; by her own hand she had slain the other for giving more affection to others. She had to think it through. Somehow it boiled down to that word mercy. She had felt cheated, and had shown no mercy. No vampire of the Dark would have blamed her for that, but she blamed herself.

What, blamed herself for not showing what she ought not to have shown? Was her thinking dull dust, her philosophy rotten at its core? Her craving to be loved went deeper. Even marriage and motherhood had eased but never satisfied it. Yet the Children of Usen—at least the chosen of his Chosen One—claimed precisely this satisfaction in quality, and a craving for ongoing quantity. They said that entering the bakery satisfied their search for bread, but not of daily bread. They said that they could not have been born with desires that couldn't in principle be met. They desired food, so logically food had to exist: would nature produce a key without a lock? Of course they might not find it, nor eat if they found it, but starvation only existed because food existed. They spoke of a love for, and from, Usen, as calling to their spirits as food called to their stomachs. Had they a core need of the spirit for love, as for food for hunger? But were vampires designed for such?

The vampires of Light said yes, but the vampires of Light were the enemy, for Light was the enemy. But what if there was a foundational love, of what all other loves, real or fancied, dimly reflected? Was Darkness not an absence of Light? Was her self-confessed need of affection a need for something deeper? Had she simply never found quite the right lock for her key? Wulfgar had found something deeper than his hold on life, and maybe Shirewude would hold that door.

Yet it was not Robin whom she sought out, he whom she had kept an eye on to restore to him his inheritance. Now she had given up that hope, realising that that had caused more trouble than it had solved. But in the watching she had picked up that virtuous as Robin was, he had been taught about mercy by Michael Tuck, whom humans prefixed as Brother, the delighter in the king's deer and loved by the good. Was it not surest to visit the source than the stream? And the stream by which that source lived she knew well, Copmanhurst.

There was a small anchorhold there, in days when forest anchorites were permitted to leave their hermitage for special mission or to supply their needs, so that the greater strictness of anchorites over hermits was not so clear cut as in towns, when anchorholds were anchored to churches as to the rock. But town or tree, anchorholds were symbolic of the scripture that the faithful have their hope anchored to the sure and steadfast rock, connected to the high priest of the inner sanctum, secure from counter-ideology's crafty currents. There dwelt Brother Tuck, safe from the seething waves of Fountains.

Well she knew that woman ought never visit anchorite alone, especially at night, even as man ought never visit anchoress alone, especially at night. Yet as woman seemed she, and she loved not the day. Shape shifting is not the piece of cake that many who cannot do it, claim it to be—at least not for vampires. It requires both refashioning of body by will, and then the fixing or freezing of that fashion. They had taken on humanoid DNA which rendered their default shape, and so did not need subjecting to their dynamic will.

And they had a portfolio of shapes that they could morph into as easily as changing a shirt. So as bat or wolf they would always look that same bat or wolf. Tweaking had to be borne in mind moment by moment, like keeping elastic stretched into an alternative shape—let it go and it will spring back to its default shape. And the weaker the vampires got, the harder to stabilise such tweaks. But Lilith was still strong of will. Voice masculinisation wasn't too difficult, nor was adding some rolls and folds to cheeks and jowl, which if body was wrapped in hooded cloak, would switch her appearance from female to male.

So it was that she as a he knocked at Tuck's door a little after midnight that night. Neither Tuck nor his dogs welcomed strangers, but a little extra knocking went a long way towards prying open his door, and she knew how to knock. With the opening of the door the dogs went unusually quiet before this black robed man, and withdrew whining to the back of the hermitage.

"Who are you?" demanded Tuck, a stout staff in hand.

"One who seeks neither food nor shelter, good hermit, only wisdom in things spiritual."

"Blessings all in good time, my son, or good buffets if we must come to blows. You seem to my eyes a hale and venerable man, but whether a wise one to disturb my prayers at this hour I know not—*medio noctis surgam*. And if not to seek spiritual wisdom, *ossa ejus perfringam*—I will break your bones, as the Holy Vulgate says."

"Peace, good hermit, for I come not in guile to entrap, but come as a Nicodemus of the night" said Lilith pacifically. "My name is Orpheus."

"Then good Orpheus, thy wanderings at night might well be understood. Yet to Hades you might fall if you mess with the Clerk of Copmanhurst. For now, prithee sit, that my hounds might regain their wits." And producing a leather bottle, he poured brimmers of ale into two drinking cups. "Waes hael" he toasted. Swiftly back came the Saxon reply, "Drink hael", for to drink well is to live well.

Ale makes hearty, and soon they were talking as fast friends. Lilith soon worked the conversation around to her point of need. Mercy seemed a strange question to Brother Tuck, whose second nature was benevolence—when not bashing heads—but by dint of question and answer Lilith began to understand it and him. Tuck wasn't perfect, and could be a self-satisfied pig among porkers though never a swine. But he had at an early age sought out the meaning of life, feeling that there must be more to life than morsels, mead, and merriment. He soon realised that each person could have purpose, but only purpose in helping others, and so people networked together.

But did anyone have meaning? He had come to see how children, too young to have value by what they could do, were loved, generally, by their parents, even as the elderly, too old to have value, could be loved by their children. Yes, that was affection—a giving not a grasping or getting. Yet he had come to see that human affection decreased as nastiness increased—the misbehaved child or parent received less affection, and might become more misbehaved by lack of affection.

Tuck had discovered that Usen, the perfect pattern, had the same affection even for the misbehaved, that indeed all his children were misbehaved in measure. He came to believe that each individual could block that affection, that love, because love's source allowed itself to be blocked, defeated, for it never forced its attention or will on any. He came to believe that no child of man had any value for Usen, since Usen did not need anything done for him—the cattle on a thousand hills were his, the wealth in every mine—but on the contrary did his utmost to give to his valueless children, though valuable still to each other. That his was an undeserved giving kind of love that offered mercy full and free, pardon to any rebel who surrendered.

This was radical talk. Mercy might be justified when the repentant rebel might be useful, but why bestow it if they had no use, and were not even of your own kind, and were prone to rebel? It made no sense, but Robin had treated Wulfgar in such mercy. Lona had not repented, was of no use, and would have turned back to her children, so had rightly been shown no mercy by the princess of Bulika, but might wrongly have been shown mercy by a human pauper! Were her wrong and right all muxed ip?

Tuck's light outshone her darkness, yet she had deemed herself the teacher. Somehow the reasoning she had used had been flawed, and it had broken her heart. Tuck had witnessed that he had received mercy at great cost to the merciful, and that in turn had moved him to show mercy, although at best he tried to balance that with an imperfect mind much divided between many clamouring commitments—how can one do right to all? The church militant had its place too. Yet even to kill the imagodei was but to transfer them from this stage to another, where perfect justice would be done unto them, as it would eventually be to their killer. His enemies here might be his friends there—*In dei minibus*, said he.

She recalled days when this new religion hadn't been running long. She had lamented that the assassination attempt had responded too slowly to slay either preborn or newborn, and that Hamashiach hadn't been killed until decades later when he should have been let be. Fact was that by the time the prophecy had been understood, he had already gone viral and the world had been changed for good.

Lilith had personally interrogated some of his new followers over the next few generations. At first these devotees had re-evaluated their citizenship. In spite of their ingrained belief that their worst fate was exclusion from their own people and from their birthright land, they risked both in a new allegiance. Many risked starvation by risking excommunication from blood communities as having become unkosher. Some sold their sacred land—as if it were no longer special—to feed their starving comrades, calling them their true kith and kin. All very countercultural! Then, against old teaching of disassociation from other races, they opened their spiritual borders to all races, all nations, and all types of people, speaking of a new commonwealth, the end of apartheid, and a new humanity in the Firstborn from Death.

At first they witnessed that they had once and for all had had their old lifestyle and thinking washed clean or at least tidied up—yet daily reminders and self-discipline seemed still to be daily routine in order to live this new way. Later on they further extended this idea of washing, suggesting that magically they could wash their children into the new kingdom—meaning nothing but good, of course. But a rash of new ideas soon sprung up, and those were interesting days that shook an Empire as new thinking was tested.

Tuck himself was rethinking some of these extended ideas that had caught on. But he did not doubt the big features of love and mercy. From the first it had been taught that Usen loved the imagodei enough to show mercy, even inviting them into the imagochristi upgrade. And in turn those accepting this invitation showed love and mercy to those of the imagodei, seeking their wellbeing even if the imagodei resented, even executed, the imagochristi. Theirs was a totally reformed idea of fatherhood, claiming to be spiritual children of their personal father: their mysterious password—αγαπωμεν αλληλου.

Would Lilith have avoided her bitterness of soul, had she taken a tip from them? Not that the tip had been on the table at that stage, or if it had she hadn't spotted it. She had once left this new people to their folly—it was not for vampires. But now she had second thoughts. Robin's mercy had taught her that good Light existed. Wulfgar had staked his life on it—but for her mercy he would have been executed. She had hoped that Wulfgar would repent of his rashness and rejoin the collective, but what if that hope was misguided? What if it was the collective which was misguided? But wasn't it true that Usen would still consign him after death to blackest hell, although he had shown mercy? Yet did not Usen and Wulfgar have mercy in common?

And yet what mercy had Usen shown in imprisoning the people of Simboliniad to Earth? Much pain they endured! But might that pain have been less if taken with a pinch of grace? Was Tuck a stream from the source? Was that source.... No, she had already gone too far. The hound of heaven bayed at her heels. Escape was gone, and she should be gone.

Having put Tuck to sleep she silently sat secluded in quiet cogitation. Would the fears of this night never finish? Her sense of control had been, was being, questioned by she herself, and she feared it soon might be by others. Self-doubt leaks out. Her single-mindedness was being tested, and her grip on her dark throne was weakening. If she fell, then two she...two whom she respected would go down with her. She had to protect them, and the only way to do that seemed to be to cast them loose. Yet that was like casting away one's anchor in a storm, only to be wrecked on a reef.

Again that idea, mercy. And that other unmentionable. And if she were deposed, what of her people who lived by her word? That would depend somewhat on who replaced her. It could be Rangda, and that could be perilous, making her people stronger yet more brittle. But

Rangda respected Draven, and if Draven sided with her she might, if queen, adopt him, in which case he could well be a moderating influence on her, protecting her people from her impetuousness. Perhaps, she thought, she should send Draven from her side, urging him to speak against her, making him more acceptable to Rangda?

As for Ishtar, she was no friend of Rangda, but at least would be spared if she had left Lilith of her own free will. Ideally that would be well before the crisis of leadership which Lilith felt now loomed large. Again, Ishtar would have to repudiate her queen. It boiled down to this: the best way to prepare her kingdom for a new monarch required the queen to secretly prepare herself and others for that. And to be even thinking along these lines, rather than fighting tooth and nail to maintain her reign, admitted that from the Night's point of view, going would best help her kingdom, and from the Dawn's point of view, staying could best help her kingdom but risked self-implosion in self-destructive violence. Having suffered a plastic deformation, Lilith lacked an elasticity to bounce back to what she had been— irreversible change. Much more pressure and she would surely snap, either into a brave new world or into diabolical tyranny.

As daylight approached, she returned as usual to her lair. As usual her daughter Ishtar and her son Draven had returned before her to the pleasant cool of the dark. That was well, for they had to talk.

"My children, my long struggle has brought me to a crisis point, a crisis for me, a crisis for our kingdom, and you must be warned and must each make a choice. The blood of Lona has long been to me as blood dried onto my hands yet seeped into my soul. Now the grave sin of Wulfgar has brought sin to my own heart and mind, a questioning about the very foundation of my throne, and my dysphoria has gone too far for safety. For I myself have shown mercy, concealed by smoke and mirrors, and that is bound to bring contention over the throne.

"In the reign of Nindara I urged the king to relinquish the throne, lest he be deposed, and now I must urge the same on myself, the queen. Shall I vacate, or vacillate until I be vanquished? You, unlike the Great Council, know that I confessed to having felt for he who was my husband and she who was my daughter. The hiding of those feelings festers, yet the revealing would have ended my reign, perhaps my life. But now maybe it should be the wider known. You must choose what is best for the kingdom. If part of my house you will fall with my house; free of family tie you could play a useful part.

"Draven, at my enthronement you spoke well of Rangda, who might well be your next queen. Rangda is strong for our weakening people, yet needs perhaps some good guidance for the good of the people. You, my son, could provide that if a prince at her side, but not as Son of Lilith. If you betrayed me to her advantage, you might well be favoured with adoption. Think therefore of winning her favour by winning my disfavour. Cast me off with the contempt I deserve, so as to guard our people.

"Ishtar, too much is your disdain for Rangda known, and adopt you she would not, nor I think would any other candidates except her adopt any cast off child of mine, if the fullness of my sins are publicly revealed. Nor I fear would you, her equal in power, be enthroned after me, for the Great Council would see through your tergiversation. Nor indeed would your brother pass that test, save perhaps in the eyes of Rangda which smile on him and frown on you.

"Herein is what little wisdom remains with me. You must both in concert defame me before the Great Council, renouncing thus your familiality with me. Play your part without praise for me. Damn me as needs be. Fear not, I will barter my throne for my life as if weary. Will they not say it is better I abdicate publicly as sapless, than be adjudged as sinner? To condemn me could condemn the kingdom." That this was unexpected was an understatement, and her children sat dazed in confusion, trying to come to grips with their mother's words. At last they spoke up, arguing that perhaps it would all pass as if nothing had happened, but as they reasoned they came to realise that her inner divergence was inexorably widening. Finally they planned their future.

Fifteen   Conspiracy

Rangda fumed. She had heard Lilith's judgement. How had it run, ah yes, "Wulfgar...your mercy...forbidden.... weakness.... Under Nindara...executed. Yet under Lilith...." Ha, under Rangda it would have been as clear cut as the line between Wulfgar's head and body! A dangerous precedent had been set. Too much was at stake to play the restoration game. Political correctness allowed no dissent to be voiced. Thrasyboulos and Tarquinius were right: if heads rise above the common herd, lob them off, for they endanger the king's head and mindset, the enthroned ideology of the day. Intelligentsia were a threat in a world where one tyranny reigned. Tall poppy syndrome kept tyrants and their thinking in post—just so long as the masses didn't arise in a flood of protest.

Rangda subscribed to a socialist realism which force-fed the masses on a strict diet of the proper ideology, forbidding contrary ideas onto the menu. Justice, justice, and justice—or injustice if that worked better and easier. Mercy should never be tolerated in a truly tolerant society. Mercy was weakness; why tolerate weakness? Weakness undermines strength. To hell with thinking that the strong ought to help the weak. Crush them! Lilith was weak; why tolerate Lilith? Rangda must undermine the throne and grab its power in bloody coup, for Lilith and her bunch would doubtless fight to the death. They should be slain anyway. To be fair, Rangda would be satisfied so long as a hardliner took the job. And with Lilith gone, no secret softliner would dare stand before the Great Council as candidate.

Yet Rangda yearned to be queen, as she had yearned once before. Why not seek it, and why not succeed? Extra kudos would gain her more votes—how could she raise her status and thereby her claim? Among many ideas one struggled to the surface: Barong must die. Rangda had long balanced her lust to harm Guardian Barong, with the fear that Usen might replace him with a mightier Kingdom Power, might imprison her for such a killing, might actually see her killed by Barong. Indeed they had had altercations before now, and so far the luck had been with Barong. In a fair fight he was like to win again. Could she get help and corner Barong into mortal combat? He had telepathic abilities, like her, but if she had enough telepaths who could block his cries for help, he would fight alone. Recent defeats still smarted.

That story ran something like this. Rangda had no affection for the secondborn, though now and again had mated with them. Recently she had had a child: the law of Nindara had only affected offspring between vampires and the firstborn. Flirtations with the senseless secondborn couldn't be significant, and tended to remain—or be born—infertile anyway. But this child had been unmarriageable, and that had vexed Rangda's pride. She kept her own affairs to herself, but some wagging tongues were saying that she had had only one child, whom some declared was a boy named Airlangga, and others retorted definitely that it was girl named Ratna Manggali.

Fools! Could they not see that if she had had one unfortunate brat, history could have repeated itself? She smiled at the rumours bandied about her. Many wiseacres even spoke of 'doublets'. That if two somewhat dissimilar accounts were circulated, too similar to be two events, but too dissimilar to be of one real event, then neither was historical, merely creative writing by storytellers. They liked the idea of Rangda having had a secondborn's child even less that Lilith having had a firstborn's child, and having two such children was two too many. Misguided were they by their prejudices, and having children by the secondborn wasn't even worth confessing to them, let alone to the Great Council.

But beautiful Ratna's exclusion from marriage had led to conflict with Durga, a Guardian queen under Usen. Under her local identity of Calon Arang, Rangda had been called a witch of black magic, a leyak, a bloodsucker, and even the queen of asuras—guessing games of the gormless! But since Calon Arang was highly feared rather than revered, surely her daughter should have been highly prized, for what man would not wish to marry into such fearsome power?

But instead Ratna had been treated like the plague. The insult to the daughter fell upon the head of her mother, and had to be repaid in blood. First Rangda had captured and drugged the local chief's daughter, intending to pass her off as her daughter unto death. Durga protected the local Children of Usen, and to her Rangda had gone seeking consent to wreak her vengeance. Over some years Rangda had feigned submission to Durga, Durga the Dimwit, as she privately called her. To this protector of humanity, Rangda blatantly boasted that her arrows of wrath would drink till they were dead drunk on her enemy's blood; that her sword would slice through their fragile flesh; that, taking no prisoners, she would sever the heads of their heads.

Well, perhaps not the most diplomatic way to gain Durga's favourable consideration, but in exchange, Rangda had offered to Durga her own child, or so she had said. Surely that special hybrid life would outweigh the merely human lives that would suffer a short burst of plague and death? Inconsequential! It also crossed her mind that if Durga did let her take revenge, possibly—and if Durga helped her, inevitably—she would slay Barong as a bonus. It would be so nice to get rid of him!

Too soon she had acted. In her pride Rangda had assumed that Durga had been deceived and delighted, and without much reflection would have readily taken the fake Ratna's life, left by Rangda in false exchange. And following that sacrifice, and the leeway it would had given Rangda for the beginning of vengeance, that maybe Durga could have been blackmailed into becoming an ally, and that together they would thus destroy Barong? In such happy bliss had Rangda gone forth, undermined the local dam, and flooded the unhappy village of Girah. Durga had beheld the floating bodies, had not been impressed by the deal of guilty for innocent, had considered a counterstroke, and released the fake Ratna.

Shortly after that a scholar named Empu Bahula, sent by a son of Rangda, had sacrificed his happiness by marrying Ratna, dying thus to save his people. After a week of wedding celebration, this Bahula discovered jottings that Rangda had made and her daughter had stolen, sketches about dethroning Lilith, *post eventum* fantasies, a diary of an ideal future, written in an unknown language which Bahula believed must be spells of black magic.

Somewhat like ornaments, vampires enjoyed making doodles or documents of victories they dreamed of, idle fancies to titivate the daylight hours, but very telling of their state of mind, and in this instance very incriminating of disloyal intention. Indeed Bahula had been advised by Rangda's son to seek out this scroll, and he believed that delivering these documents to the great and powerful Durga would lead to Rangda's permanent expulsion from the kingdom.

For superstitious Bahula believed that exposing black magic spells allowed white magic to overcome them. Little did he cotton on that they were actually proof of high treason in heart and mind, proof which would have allowed Durga to blackmail Rangda into submission.

In folly he had sent these accounts not unto Durga but unto his lord—to protect against another *pralaya*—but it was not done without Rangda's knowledge. To her hatred of Airlangga's marriage, she added her fear of public exposure, and had sought earnestly to regain the documents or to reduce them to ashes. Against her son's kingdom she had gathered diaboloi from the jungle to assist. Airlangga, having to face off against his own mother to save his kingdom, had called on Durga for help, and she had sent brobdingnagian Barong, Durga choosing not to directly ally with the House of Airlangga.

A fearsome fight had been fought, and against Barong and the many aggeloi at his command, Rangda and her forces had both inflicted and suffered loss. Neither side had exactly won, but in the end the incriminating documents had simply vanished from the face of the earth. Perhaps those dwellers of the deep below the knowledge of light, those of Nidavellir, had taken them from Airlangga. Whatever, they were gone and neither Rangda nor Durga were any the wiser. Finally, Rangda, hurt and humiliated, had run away to fight again another day.

That was then. Now that day of vengeance was coming. Rangda was thinking it through. Barong would die, but she would need help. One recently resurfaced dunamos was Mahishasura. Not to be confused with the long gone king Mahisha, the dunamos Mahisha was indeed a fallen Asura, and one who had in various forms fought over ten millennia against Durga, so closely matched had they been, before being to all appearances killed. His head had been cut off, but his inner essence had flown from it in the nick of time, and had lain as a chrysalis for centuries beyond count. But now it had again taken form, and bore no love for Durga and her minions, among whom Barong sat in high honour. Other powerful asuras of the Dark there were, who issuing from the dynamic bubble had at first sided with the Light, only turning to their dark shadow-self in later ages. Now if

Danu and her son Vritra, say, joined with her, why, even Durga would not be able to save Barong.

But then, to maximise her chance of the throne, she really had to be seen to destroy Barong herself. Once invited to the party, holding Danu and Vritra back could prove a headache. Yet if mother and son lent her their tertiaries, their foot soldiers, keeping the big names out of battle, well, she could defeat Barong with their help yet boast his death by her hand. But perhaps just one dunamos to ensure victory? Yes, and for her part she would promise that if ever the Necros in turn needed help, as queen she would be open to alliance. To make it work she was prepared to do a deal with Necuratu himself.

Thus it was that she secretly summoned all the evil spirits in the jungle, both demons and *corrumpi*—leyaks, as the unquiet dead (often mistaken for diaboloi) were called, who with the demons helped spread disease and death in the kingdom. Leading the diaboloi was Mahishasura, keen not for a rematch with Durga, but to aid in the downfall of Barong, unfortunate favourite of his queen. And coaxing out Barong had always been too easy. For he walked safely in the surety of his own might—a might mighty indeed—with help at his beck and call. But this day he walked unsafely without his monkey guard. He walked unsafely, into a trap well laid.

There had always been the chance that one time his own might might not suffice. It only took one time, and this was the time. Rangda herself lured him out, then lured him away as a sheep to be slaughtered, as a lion to be shorn then slain. For she, going alone into a village, by hallucinations caused self-harm and suicide among its protectors, and in the chaos the people cried out for rescue.

Hearing their cry, Barong came rushing in as a roaring lion, to the left and the right suffusing the inflicted with power to resist even the keris they were using to self-harm or self-destruct, and to the front springing straight at Rangda. But as a horrendous hag Rangda turned and fled, and as a lion Barong pursued through wood and air. Now while it is true that the divinities sometimes gathered at Di Hyang, they dwelt not there, and it was now to this safe place that Rangda led Barong that day. And there, in that mountainous area of sunless smoke and sickening sulphur, high up above the sea, the trap was sprung. For lesser spirits beyond count encircled, hidden far beyond sight of the lava dome on which she landed. And Mahishasura himself came forth as a gigantic buffalo, to the dismay of Barong. Now Mahishasura on his right, Rangda on his left; next Mahishasura before him, and Rangda behind him.

Barong cried loud is desperation, but his cry went unheard, silenced by the surrounding spirits. He slashed at his enemies, claws of ripping power. Rangda fell back in searing pain, and would never be the same. Bolts of blue light came from his paws, and both his foes cried out in stabbing pain, but bolts of power they returned with a vengeance, and he too knew pain. He tried to flee, but shields of power blocked his retreat, as diaboloi and leyaks opposed his flight. Encaged, he turned determined to harm the evil before him before yielding up his life: it would be dearly bought.

Weakened, wounded, and weary, Mahishasura withdrew on Rangda's command. Until then she had played but minor fiddle, encouraging Barong to expend his defence on Mahishasura. Now Rangda, scarred but not scared, had the upper hand, for Barong was almost broken, and not much more was needed to deliver the *coup de grâce* which would finally put an end to Barong's misery, but not for mercy's sake. Still fresh she played him out. His bolts of power, now ebbing, she pretended were great, while her own bolts felt soft but looked severe. Thus she eked out Barong's agony, while feigning to fight one equal still in strength, enhancing thus her ultimate victory. Killing cruelly she effaced her many defeats at his hands.

Fallen, fallen is Barong the Great! At least four other spirits there were who had played lesser Barongs—Asu, Bangkal, Gajah, and Macan. Their leader Ket had now fallen and gone to his eternal reward, but his apprentices would continue the good fight in his name. As to his current state of being, Rangda neither knew nor cared, for her joy was in his defeat at her hands, and the plaudits that could accrue to her. Yet she strangely felt a double-edged loss at his loss—never again could she grieve in her defeats, but never again could she revel in their fights. But time to move on. From Durga she was safe. Durga would probably never know how Barong was lost, not that that mattered, for even if she discovered the truth she was not such as would seek revenge.

Rangda returned without fanfare, keeping her triumph to herself. Having enhanced her own claims to the throne, she sought out other potential claimants. They were but few. Abchanchu the Violent was deceptive, and might well make a play for the post. Empusa of the Shining Foot was another, who had been adopted by the Guardians as daughter to Hekatē, but had proved wayward to their teachings. Jilaiya of the Name was up to it, though not outstanding. Yarama-yhawho of the Head, just maybe, but he was a bit odd and was slow at coming forward. Yukinba of the Snow had a definite sadistic streak, yet at times released her toys—she could still go far. Yet Rangda of the Fangs fancied her chances among these, especially when she would play her trump card as Barong's Bane! Fortunately Lamaštu wouldn't run in any race for the throne, for she had happily settled into Necuratu's kingdom—you didn't want to mess with her. So Abchanchu, Empusa, Jilaiya, Yarama-yhawho, and Yukinba, were probably the only interested parties to plan with to unseat Lilith.

And so it was that she secretly networked with them in twos or threes, sowing seeds of discontent, seeds of no confidence in the queen. Besides Lilith's leniency upon Wulfgar, his name was singled out to argue that the vampires needed to become more like the Necros: had not Lamaštu been touched by the might of Darkness, Wulfgar by the madness of Light? The vampires of Light remained a thorn in the side. Greater convergence with the diaboloi would allow a decisive extirpation of these delinquents. Why did the queen not lead her people into total victory? Why was she content with the status quo? New direction was needed, new thinking, new courage. With any luck a spirit of discontentment would creep into the Great Council.

And speaking of luck, extraordinary news was leaking out that Lilith's own children were unhappy with her treatment of Wulfgar, and were urging her to reverse her leniency and to have him secretly assassinated. When challenged by Abchanchu they had seemed awkward and denied it, but it could well be that on the one hand they wished to shield their mother from the public admission of wrongdoing—which an order of execution would involve—while on the other hand ensuring that Wulfgar nevertheless paid with his life.

How the leak had started was uncertain, but it could even be that one of them had deliberately let it slip, preparing the ground for a decisive break with her. Anyway this seemed a stroke of good fortune, and Rangda could certainly capitalise on it. As for Ishtar, she could go jump in the deepest sea, for all Rangda cared—they had had their run-ins. But as for Draven, why, he had once slightly slighted her by preferring Lilith, but he had been objective. Yet if now he agreed with her over Lilith, perhaps was even playing with the idea of leaving family, why, maybe they could do some mutual back-scratching: *domus mea domus tua*. She would sound him out without delay.

And so it was that Rangda soon had a word in Draven's shell-like ear, over a concern which she and a few other leaders of influence, she said, shared *apropos* Lilith's fitness to reign—though all of course would support Lilith to the hilt, she added. In other words, she lied through her back teeth. Draven was no fool, nor did she seek one, and as she intended he instantly understand her true message to him: a power struggle must take place—which side would he support? And—he let her to understand that he had already given his options some thought—he was prepared to switch allegiance, but only if Rangda gave him assurances that if possible neither Ishtar nor Lilith would be harmed, an assurance quickly given. Lowering his voice he said, "I have discovered a secret of secrets that can cause her doom, but she has reigned well and should for the wellbeing of the kingdom be allowed to retire gracefully."

"I would rather she be dragged down as a wounded stag," said Rangda with some heat, "but it could cause contention if she fights for her throne, so I will comply. But what dirt have you got on her?" Rangda's curiosity was piqued, and she also realised that she could personally assassinate Lilith at a convenient time, probably best without Draven's foreknowledge. Both boxes would be ticked, simply a case of deferring the one marked death.

"It is the knowledge of high treason, but your word that both Ishtar and I may disown Lilith before this spreads. If we perish with her, many more will perish in civil war, but if used as blackmail Lilith will go quietly. She has already said that a reason for releasing Wulfgar was to prevent civil war, so how could she now invoke war to save her throne? Her former reason would be seen as spurious, mere mercy, and her allies would desert her." So it was that under guise of disgust and disloyalty, Draven fed the information which Lilith had commissioned him to betray. And Rangda took the bait, hook, line, and sinker, and all but took the throne.

Knowledge is power, it is said, and Rangda felt empowered. The rest is now somewhat history. She had sought a private audience, and facing Lilith alone had disclosed the information she had obtained—from a confidential but reliable source, she said. Lilith had bowed her head, and swiftly to save her kingdom she admitted defeat. She expected no pardon, nor asked for it. She had done wrong, but best to make it right by abdicating. Thus it was before the Great Council that they soon stood. She declared that she had great weariness as queen, that it was too much for her, and that she remained a powerful supporter of the darker side of the vampire kingdom. Asked who she would most see on the throne, she endorsed Rangda.

Of Abchanchu, Empusa, Jilaiya, Yarama-yhawho, and Yukinba, only Abchanchu, Empusa, and Yukinba, stood forth as candidates. Jilaiya and Yarama-yhawho saw that with Lilith's endorsement, Rangda was too strong to stand against. Then Draven stood up, and endorsed Rangda, whom he had just heard had killed mighty Barong. At first his endorsement carried little weight on the grounds of bias, since he had recently been adopted by Rangda: presumably he had been released by Lilith just prior to her abdication. But when he mentioned Barong, why, if that were true, then he spoke of a mighty turnaround in the fortunes of war.

Long had it been known that Barong had had the upper hand over Rangda. Witnesses to this claim were immediately called for and questioned, after which two who had stood stood no more. Yukinba on their right, and Rangda on their left: the Great Council would vote. Rangda had endorsement from the outgoing queen as well as a recent and highly meritorious victory, and had stood before. Yukinba had much to her credit, but playing with her toys, even though without mercy, carried some uncertainties. Those who become monarch must put away both childish and diabolical things. The Great Council closed eyes and cut. Slashes to the left, all save one; slashes to the right, one, no abstentions. What more needed to be said, save "Hail Rangda, queen of the vampires. Long live the queen!"

Sixteen KAINOS KOSMOS

Following her ascension, Rangda dropped all talk about realignment with the Necros, but let her co-conspirators know that she had previously made a pact of willingness. That raised questions in their minds about what help the Necros might have afforded her in the overcoming of Barong. Perhaps her prowess was not as they had been led to believe! They had already wondered about how Lilith had so meekly abdicated, all but handing Rangda the throne on a platter—had some kind of skulduggery tricked them?

But these were not of humankind, that they should resent having been cheated. To them craftiness was a virtue, and craft on the throne was the way to rule. 'As sneaky as a serpent and as wounding as a wolf', was an axiomatic proverb. And Rangda had known that it was wiser to let the cat out of the bag, than to let it scratch and squeak until discovered: don't react, proact! Her co-conspirators were now her supporters, her colleagues, not her rivals, and were content. After her ascension she adopted Yukinba, in part for her sheer audacity in facing up to her in the election. Yukinba could prove useful in the assassination of Lilith, for that remained an old score to settle, an old sore to soothe.

Unexpectedly Ishtar had just had a private interview with Rangda. Ishtar, no longer a daughter, had read Rangda's mind, seeing Lilith's death in her eyes, and bluntly informed Rangda that although she, Ishtar, had reneged on family bonding since the hiatus about Wulfgar, yet she would not stand idly by and see a precedent set of a former sovereign secretly slain. Rangda had smiled to herself, thinking it'd be rather difficult to know that a secret precedent hadn't already been set had it been always kept secret, but forced her mind back to what Ishtar was saying.

She was being challenged to either demand a public execution, or to kill Lilith over Ishtar's dead body: put up or shut up. Awkward alternatives. Two such ladies was one too many for Rangda to handle. That's why the idea of Yukinba looked so attractive. Even so it was probably best to let revenge fester, awaiting a more propitious time to strike when their guard was down, maybe one at a time. Curse Ishtar, that interfering old busybody.

∞

Ishtar flew to visit Lilith in her self-exile, her hermitude. "Hail Lilith, once mother in law, still mother in heart."

"Ishtar, welcome. But it is unwise to visit me thus, unless you come as an emissary", said Lilith in all seriousness. "I do not imagine that the queen will leave me long in peace, and doubt not that she plans dark death for me. She who has taken my throne, what can she now take but my life? You I know will not be her knife, but I fear lest it bear your name too."

"Too late I think for fear, but I visit nonetheless" replied Ishtar. "Doubt not that she hides a knife for us twain, yet fears to use it openly, the more because I have declared to her my alliance to you. She yearns your death, but must now include mine, and so her need of allies grows. Draven she must know would stay her hand, but her daughter would welcome such a death fight. Yet Rangda must surely see that her chances are few unless she gains other help, and that the more there are who know her plot, the harder to hide it or deny it. But I have not come to speak of fear."

"Then what is your errand, my friend?" asked Lilith. There was a momentary pause, the taking of breath before taking the plunge.

"Lilith, for millennia I knew of your love for he who was your husband, and for she you slew as daughter, and of your grief at their loss. And your grief you accounted shame. Draven too felt it shame, yet remained loyal to you as to a leader of high honour and justice. You were ever thankful of such, and assumed that I shared not such shame and so passed over yours as did Draven the Unashamed. But did you never wonder whether I, playing as it seemed with men, had no real regard for them? Did you think that you alone could suffer such a weakness, such a shame, of care? Did you never ask whether in fact it was a source of shamelessness, not of shame?

"At first I too doubted myself, taught as we are to deride feelings of affection, fearing to feel the conflict which was the downfall of Wulfgar. We are taught that such stirrings are wrong, but what if it is our teaching that is wrong and affection and mercy that are right? What if this heresy should be orthodox, a thing of glory and not of shame? With the death of Gilgamesh I felt my deepest loss, and shame too to lament his death in secret as if a hidden sin. How could I weep unless weeping is according to nature? What if my true nature was in accord to nature, and not twisted nature? Surely the ought exists—or else there is no *ought* behind concern for our own people, and without an ought there would be but chaos, each trampling over the weaker until all but one are trampled underfoot. And that ultimate vampire would be powerfully alone. Is dog eat dog the goal of life—if goal there be—or is it but a gaol of the soul?

"For millennia I kept my doubts to myself, until the recent news broke of a man of the secondborn having defeated death itself, a power far beyond us. Was it fake news? It was heralded that he had been the prophesied one, Hamashiach, he whom we had so long striven to kill, knowing that he would not be deathless. Yet it was told that he himself had prepared the ground, selected the field of battle, the place of the scull, then summoned death to fight to the death. It was told that in their struggle he was killed by death, yet not without having mortally wounded death and freeing humanity from death's grip. From his blood a new people arose from the earth in his wake, facing death in his name as sheep to the slaughter, yet seeking a joy that was set before them. Should we who stave off death at all cost, account these who embrace death as lesser? Are not these ephemeral mortals a sign to us of hope? In appearance as a woman I spoke with them.

"Of his new people of the Krismic Kingdom—those called by some the Anōthen—those of the city of Kolossai explained to me that Huion Prōtotokon is beyond the creation of time, is, under Usen, lord of the very heavenly cosmos which in him is supported by him, yet he shone forth in a shape, becoming a cosmic creature, Hamashiach, to save the secondborn, visualising Usen the Invisible to those who would see. Is there not chaos within the universe which shattered Simboliniad? Is there not chaos within this world? Yet is there not an order transcendent? I asked myself: Might he who came here from beyond time and space, care also for us who came here merely from time and space, even as he does for Usen's children of this world, if as Hamashiachim say, all things have been created unto him? Did he not voluntarily become imprisoned for all time? Is he our true orientation, however disorientated we be in our twisted nature?

"They claimed that many of their number had been disorientated, rebels twisted in head, heart, and hand, yet had been made new creatures with the new Image. Many lessons were they given, lessons for them to learn, but not for us I deem, though their revelation speaks I think of us as on a converging road, as a flock that will one day join the fold, of insights even to the vampires of Dawn long sundered. Lilith, as you I have wept, but have now found peace. I am of Hamashiach. You who seek, will you not find?"

Lilith stood in awe. Quietly, she replied that she too have spoken with those of the Anōthen, those of The Way. Once when in the pay of Gaius Plinius Caecilius Secundus, and once before. But such interest was dangerous and kept secret. Never before had any vampire voluntarily put their mortal life into her hands, though she had once offered her life to her children, and again for her kingdom. But to receive can be more blessèd, and harder, than to give.

Ishtar was offering Lilith two options. One, she could surrender to Usen in Hamashiach and become a Hamashiachi, as was Ishtar. Two, she could surrender Ishtar into the hands of Rangda and the Great Council. That betrayal would earn Lilith both pardon and praise. What forbidden love was this, that Ishtar would lay down her life for her friend? Love was not allowed on the menu—Ishtar had eaten forbidden fruit. Since for showing mercy Wulfgar had deserved death, how much more Ishtar—unless she was right to love? Was love according to nature?

Among the spirits of deep heaven, some claimed that Usen was Love, the very source and correction of creaturely loves. Guardians Meslamtæa and Ereshkigal had told her something like that in the days of Nindara, much to his annoyance. She had never personally killed a vampire of Light, and now was glad that she had not, if Light was right. Yet she had never revoked the command to kill them on sight, but *realpolitik* would have made revocation impossible anyway, short of a substantial sea change. But what should she do about Ishtar? Pursue her belief, or persecute it?

To persecute would bring her power, and also remove one who knew of her wayward heart, her—from the Night's perspective—sinfulness. Then only Rangda and Draven would know, and Rangda's knowledge was only second-hand, although substantially confirmed by the blackmail affect it had had on Lilith. Not to betray Ishtar would leave Lilith exposed to sure death if the truth of her knowledge ever came out. To join Ishtar would be to commit to the Day in the sure and certain knowledge of the committal unto death. For Lilith knew that she could never be a secret believer: her people would be her people no more, and she would be killed unless she escaped. Was Hamashiach for her, or would she fall a fool between stools? Yet if there was even a chance, a chance to rid her dark soul of its dark blot, a chance to get right with herself, to affirm her nature according to nature....

And thus she took the plunge and surrendered defeated. Better to die now than to live later. And Hamashiach saw and stepped in. She saw as in a vision her long departed world, saw again the crystal joy, but now she saw it as a joy which pointed beyond itself, a taster, a *terminus a quo*, not a *terminus ad quem*.

She glimpsed next the very face of the lucifer, the phōsphoron who, even like as Venus to Earth begins the hours of day, had begun a new day as if a bright morning star shining forth the radiance of Usen's face, enlightening his true children. And much profound exploration she saw beyond of the telescopic and the microscopic, when the ultimate Children of Usen, free from both gravity's shackles and need for machines, roamed around the universe, as if a playground of infinite wonder. Wonders indescribable, untameable, unending. And a loving warmth she felt that her erotic and motherly loves had softly hinted at. This warmth was of an unsentimental no nonsense love that cut to the heart, and would be sure and certain death to all evil if permitted. A love that saw beyond death but violated not, yea rather enhanced and fulfilled life, and loved her. And she wept.

Yes, she wept, and Ishtar wept with her. Before, they had wept tears of bitterness, having been Mara not Naomi. Now Lilith wept tears of release, and Ishtar wept tears of empathy. They hugged. In their dark cavern they hugged as sisters, sisters in a secret hope, a secret joy, a secret fellowship. The leaden load had lifted, and even as the spring rain falls sweetening the ground for the sun, so their falling tears lasted not overlong.

Her cave was somehow different, as if some uncanny illumination lit its dark recesses, some illumination which seemed to creep into Lilith. She positively glowed! Only the foolish would have imagined that she had been her usual self-sustaining self, just prior to that visitation. Deposed, she had stoically, sadly, awaited her inevitable fate. Thoughts of gloom had been hers; the black dog of the night had become her faithful pet and constant companion. The judgement of Usen had played around her head, that meeting of all meetings the most to be feared. Now she had met him in life, not through death, and the meeting had been of all meetings the most ravishing, and the end was not yet. She rose and went forth into the sunshine. Eyes, once hurt by the light, having seen the wondrous face of the lucifer, now welcomed the created light, as if itself a pale foreshadowing of the light of lights, the father of lights, he who is more reliable, more illuminating, than the cosmos itself. Hers was a whole new cosmos.

And Ishtar went with her, for they were not out of the woods yet— assassination or assimilation was in the air. "Lilith my sister, now I must train you in the ways of underground believers," began Ishtar, "for it might be that Rangda will sheath her knife, content to merely gnash on her anger until toothless she be. Therefore prudence dictates that we keep our heads down, speak only as the Dark speak, and speak ill of Wulfgar. Thus maybe the anger of the queen will disperse and we may live in peace. As to our diet, the Children of Usen should be spared, yet I have found that other creatures there are that will suffice, if drained in good grace."

"Ishtar, there is doubtless much you can teach me about the new way, a way familiar to you, but shall I keep my head down, I whose head was once crowned? Strange questions come to my mind unsought, which I must answer. Who knows whether it was for a time like this that I became queen? Does Usen, who has spoken to me, seek to speak now to our blinded people? If I do not give him voice, will liberation and protection come to them from other lips, and will we perish by the hand of Rangda? For we cannot always be on guard, nor always walk this road together. If she bides her time, stalks our movements, will she not strike first one, then the other? But if we face the Great Council, why, our lives will be forfeit or freed, and if freed the queen will not overrule and we shall live free. And if we face the Great Council, it may be that it will hear and heed the words of Usen. Ishtar, could it not be that a new day will dawn for our people?"

Ishtar was not sanguine. "It comes to my mind that this is not the year of redemption, if ever that year shall come, but perhaps in the dying we shall at least sow its seed. I would be craven to desert you to your fate, solely to save my own skin. Therefore, if I cannot persuade you to change your course, I will take it with you. Perhaps Ishtar too came to be a princess for such a time as this."

Thus it was that they took the plunge, and sought not audience with the queen—lest their words be concealed and their lives be taken by concealed fangs in the dark—but with the Great Council itself. But for Draven's adoption to new princedom, he would have been translated to the council on Lilith's abdication. Yet as a prince he had right to enter the Great Council whenever it met, as had Rangda and Yukinba. As a former princess, Ishtar had of course been offered a place by right, but had declined for personal reasons unstated. Sage heads had nodded, reckoning simply that, having deserted Lilith for shame at her weakness, she needed time alone. No matter, the post remained open indefinitely. The voices of Draven and Ishtar on the council would have been powerful friends, yet at best a minority report questioned by the unbiased. Yet now only Ishtar's voice would be heard, and that through Lilith, though she would be standing in front of the bench.

Gjaku stood, as did the other members of the Great Council. For Lilith and Ishtar had been former queen and princess respectively, and were worthy of highest honour. "We, the Great Council, are gathered to hear why we have been summoned." With that he bowed low and sat down.

Lilith arose. "Gjaku, Great Council, Queen, Prince, Princess, I Lilith greet you, and claim right of silent hearing before judgement. Behold, I bring you good news of great joy for all our people. But know who I am. For behold, I was as queen guilty of charges unknown. For you thought my sin merely one of marriage, and that pardonable. Know now that it was of love, a thing forbidden, but a thing in our nature repressed. For does it not come from Usen, and do we not rebel against him and his? Yet is not our nature of his creating, and are we to rebel against our own nature? If we are bound by him to this world, are we not bound by our hatred to the despite of our nature? If but one is wrong, which is it?

"In pride I did take the life of Lona, once daughter to me, and grieved secretly—for grieving we account a sin. But I have asked myself, should mercy not have withheld my hand? Know now that my mercy for Wulfgar was not merely for the kingdom, but somewhat in atonement for my withholding mercy from Lona the Lost. Yet know too that Wulfgar is not of Hamashiach, and went forth with inner diaboloi. Yet are we, in as we claim balanced affinity with them, not enslaving ourselves as much as he? Can we not find freedom from the Black Hand? Behold, I have come to see that Usen offers pardon even to the people from Simboliniad, and that it is for purpose undisclosed that he has enslaved us to this world.

"The Rock is perfect, and all his ways are just: unjustly have we called him unjust. Our people slowly weaken, even as do our eyes. Yet in turning my heart and mind towards Usen, my eyes have been strengthened and the light once painful has become the light of promise. Is this not gain? Should you not rejoice my good fortune? Surely tidings of great joy for all our people?

"Ishtar stands with me, and we stand with Hamashiach, returned from death, and before him we stand. Pronounce therefore your doom. Before this court our blood can be shed. But will that either avail our people or blind them? Will they not seek out the truth of our martyrdom? Or take for yourselves words of hope, and with them let us proclaim their message throughout the kingdom. Is it of no consequence in your sight that I, who have dwelt a counsellor to Nindara, and queen to our people, have with great boldness offered my life to you this day, and speak of joy new found? And not only I but Ishtar, once princess? Or cast us forth as heretics most foul, and leave us be in our own folly." With that Lilith sat down besides Ishtar.

The council carefully considered its verdict. Telepathically it networked its reflections, blocking out all others. It was said that such fools were like a virus, and that it was not fit that they should live. It was said that possibly, just possibly, Usen had spoken to them, but then again maybe a mischievous spirit had spoken to vex the vampires? Yet Lilith looked better than ever and in her right mind: would a diaboloi make her so? Usen had once trapped them to Earth; did he speak again to entrap them—what further evil had he hidden up his sleeve? Was he not in fact the most mischievous of elohim, though death to the diaboloi?

The council must not be taken in, must hear no more of Usen. To let Lilith loose upon the people was never going to fly. Some would believe such nonsense; the virus would multiply among the weak-minded, endanger them all. To converse with her would be a sheer waste of time—she had become a babbling fool proclaiming some kind of resurrection, as crazed as they who still said that the earth was flat.

Ishtar stood in agreement. It would be just to execute them both, but that could be to make martyrs out of them: some would ask that since a lie is not worth dying for, might they have preached the truth? Not a safe question for public discussion. Perhaps the least divisive option was to banish them for unforgivable sin, a verdict not open to renegotiation. A charge of caring for humanity would suffice, and linked to their assignations with the Children of Usen, would harden the line that his children should be out of bounds to vampires, a health hazard. Don't play with your food!

Gjaku and the Great Council stood, but this time with their backs to Lilith and Ishtar. In a voice of unison, their minds perfectly melded, they uttered words of exclusion, or repulsion, of damnation.

"Lilith, Ishtar, dishonoured beyond repentance, hear ye now your fate. Banished for ever are you from your people of the Night. Spared your lives are but not saved—banished you are. Cut off to wither and die alone—banished you are. Neither saving nor succour shall be yours from the Night—banished you are. Go from us, never to return—banished you are. If we meet again it shall be on the field of battle—banished you are.

"Any who side with you shall be cut off from the Dark Side—banished you are. Speak not to us but go, for your words are words of death to us—banished you are. Never again shall you stand before the Great Council—banished you are. All rights are revoked beyond recall—banished you are. Depart from us, evil doers—banished by extraction you are."

One by one each member raised their voice in lament, in rage, in savagery. The psychic shock-wave would resound throughout the kingdom. All would hear within of the repugnance of Lilith and Ishtar. All intercourse would be ended from that day forth. The miscreants were as dishonoured dead to their people, unburied, unmourned, and meaningless. And Lilith and Ishtar left without Parthian shot, rejoicing that they were counted worthy to suffer shame for Hamashiach's name.

Seventeen Banished and Free

The ordeal was over, and the two friends and sisters left at leisure. By a banishment of extraction, the ultimate repudiation, the Great Council had removed them from the rights, responsibilities, and revenge, of the Night. Don't misunderstand: they intended no mercy, but were merely being pragmatic. With numbers and strength depleting, why waste resources by leaving the malefactors open to assassination? For too often had well meaning assassins of the Night been assassinated, wasted—and what good was that?

And so Lilith and Ishtar had been set free to move into the protective cover of the vampires of Dawn—or wherever they wished: the Great Council simply said that they were damned if they cared! Lilith and Ishtar were now untouchables, as long as they didn't directly interfere with the business of the Night. They had spoken out boldly and proclaimed the word of Usen to the Great Council. That word had been thrust away, as words on a parchment heard then burnt as rubbish, as if the council had judged itself unworthy of the eternal Light. Now the friends turned towards the vampires of Dawn.

Over the next few hundred years they spoke to every vampire they could find who self-identified with the Dawn. Unlike with easily misled humans especially in youth, for vampires, self-identifying was not self-harming, but true identifying, meaningful not mutilation. They found that these vampires all shared certain characteristics. For one thing, they all wrestled to a certain extent with the Eighth Law. Why had it been imposed? Why should Usen value freedom yet imprison them?

Some resolved the problem by saying that since Usen was Goodness, then the Eighth Law was deliberately bad in order to test their sincerity to him. "Imagine on the one hand," Zima had said, "that Usen had from the outset fenced our enemies out. And then that he had blessed all we did and spread us throughout the cosmos. Would any of us have turned from him? No! But would our gratitude have invoked any real commitment, even love? Imagine on the other hand that Usen had from the outset fenced us in, clipping our wings that wished to fly, curbing our powers. 10Would we not curse him to his face? Yes! But if any praised his name, would they not be only those who through trial and tribulation have passed into meaningful loyalty and love? Only if the princess loves the frog does she get the prince. So we love him not because of, but in spite of, and is that not true love?" She was content to love without understanding, leaving all in the lap of Usen. Of the last allusion Zima had spoken of a frog, but in fact it had definitely been a toad which a Dark vampire, living incognito as a human prince, had once shape shifted into. In fact Ishtar had played a secret part for the happy couple. Well, stories from the Night Kingdom sometimes got twisted in the telling.

Still, back on track Zima, along with her companions, wondered if the trying test of loyalty was ever going to end, but with or without hope they had faith, faithfulness. Meeting up with Bonifacio, they discovered some reasoned hope: "if shackled we love him, surely, his love and liberty being source, he intends that we will love him more in freedom?" He was a philosopher, was Bonifacio. And they found among these vampires that, as with themselves, daylight was no longer a danger. That was good, because it meant that they less often met with the Night, and so risk was reduced. Different trajectories led to distant tension.

So light was another thing in common, as was love, as was a positive attitude towards their bondage. And another difference. Theirs was not a bondage to decay. Even the innately weaker vampires, such as Zima, had grown somewhat in power since accepting their fate with a smile instead of a snarl. When of the Night, they had fearfully felt their fading power which alone held back their fate. The Dark vampires were a morbid lot, really. Not a thing you noticed when within that kingdom, but switching sides made a heaven of a difference. One thing they had expected in common but did not find. Both Lilith and Ishtar had assumed that human blood would be unkosher—but it was not.

As Umi had put it: "Usen's secondborn kill each other for many different reasons, counting life but cheap. Usen moreover has created wolves and big cats that feast on human flesh. It is not sacrosanct, for both he and humans protect these animals. So surely if we went to war we would be permitted to take human life? And if we go not to war with the secondborn, what lesser harm is it to take one here or there for our sustenance? So, they who would die soon die sooner, the sooner meet their eternal reward or retribution: either way will they bewail mortal years cut short? Besides, we who partake seldom drink to the dregs. Can they not spare blood for good cause?" He added that what was not of good conscience was subjectively sin, so that although he had no problems with feeding on human life and blood, he would never urge conscientious objectors to partake, for that would defile community conscience and cheapen them all. Many, however, were as Ishtar had long been, content to hunt lesser prey.

Faramundo was a kindred spirit. He was to all intents and purposes a secondborn, serving as a chief of guard from common stock. He was content to be good, and was highly respected by his lord. His fighting skills of course exceeded the human level, but he underplayed his skills to keep under cover. He had had questions about Hamashiach, whom some had said was an outlaw, but tended to assume that whatever he was, he was not for vampires to bother with. Lilith and Ishtar tended to go about in appearance as old crones, not worth a second look, not worth being molested.

Often one vampire or group would have an idea about where another lived, and the two Hamashiachim would be directed there, telepathically announcing their presence when they arrived. And close up there was something in a vampire's eyes that their own people could always spot. It was good that they had been directed to Faramundo. On meeting, he had sat down with them alongside the Tiberis River. They had become disheartened, for the Dawn Kingdom seemed happy not to upgrade into the Day Kingdom, since it needed not redemption.

Seven days in the sunshine they sat and spoke. He listened, and questioned them. The themes of mercy and of love he knew and respected. And the fear of death was not a big deal for him. His heart was right with Usen, for he walked in the Dawn. As for Hamashiach, the avatar of Huion, he was just for Usen's children, wasn't he? The aspect of forgiveness took time, not to say but to get across. At the end of the seven days Lilith, searching for words, seemed herself to gain insight. "It is not simply letting you off, Faramundo, it is letting you in. Think rebellion not simply as an offense to be overlooked, nor justice as blindly bought off by another's unjust payment of life—as if justice cares for retribution but not whether guilty or innocent carry the can.

See rebellion as a blockage barring a city gate. See that Usen's forgiveness is removing that which blocks you from entering in."

"But what rebellion have I that blocks my way? Am I not of the Dawn?" he asked.

"Faramundo," replied Ishtar, "Lilith has spoken of blockage. Is your mind not itself the blockage? If his will is for you to enter deeper—to live in Hamashiach's city rather than in Usen's fields—is your will to not enter not rebellion against his will, rebellion that needs release? But as only those who see their sin can see their saviour, so only if you see your resistance as rebellion can you see the need to surrender to his unblocking of your will. Asking forgiveness is asking to go through the gate into his inner kingdom, and all who seek shall find."

Faramundo had sat quietly, pondering. "We of the Dawn find it hard to understand the ways of Usen, and we seek to delve deeper, as do the very aggeloi. Is it that the answer is to be found deeper in and higher up, a journey we are loth to take, a price too high to pay? Is it that only with the coming of Hamashiach can we understand the why of the Eighth Law?"

"Yes," said Lilith, "our people of the Dawn need fear not beyond death, but before death can find new life and explanation only by entering Hamashiach's kingdom. By saying that you have no need, you deceive yourself and the truth is not yet in you. By admitting the truth of your need, you can receive Hamashiach and be received."

Faramundo bowed his head, processing the information. He sensed his pride, his self-reliance, his own admittedly good nature. Yet he sensed also his need, his lack of spiritual exploration, his passivity to time. Here were witnesses, watchers, who had surely met one they had once sought to slay. They had come out of the Dark Side into the Day, into light brighter than he had known, a higher level. They invited him to bow to new management, to new insight, to a new relationship and fellowship.

Finally he bowed his head in surrender, receiving the gift of Hamashiach. He raised his head. His eyes that told that he was a vampire, now told that he was also a Hamashiachi. Questions he asked, and answers they gave. Some answers they had not, and he would have to wait. But answers were coming. Before they left he asked if he might join them in their travel, and they were pleased.

That day he presented himself before his lord and begged leave to depart. Having served with honour he left with the livery of the castle and his sword and shield.

It was not that none of the Dawn had become Hamashiachim. Some had been such for over a millennium, but it was still a relatively new idea, and truth be told most of the Dawn had become complacent in their own goodness, the light they had already received. They were not of the damned, but little bothered with digging deeper: one day Usen would explain it to them, they said. And they said right: but better to know without waiting than to wait without knowing. Still it was their choice—that of remaining high on zeal but rather weak on understanding.

As the three now travelled about, Faramundo now travelled in the guise of a protector. And that was not remiss, for although the Night had washed its hands of them, the Necros wasn't done with them yet. Yet now there were three vampires of the Day, and all three were among the mighty. And so they travelled in safety.

As the years rolled on, Faramundo and Ishtar found ever more comfort in each other, and moreover felt that their mission was to one of the Night, whereas Lilith felt that hers was to settle down and wait near to the forest of Shirewude—and there was someone she particularly wished to see. Thus it was that they went different ways, even as the two sisters had once diverged to hunt for different game. Long ago did those days above the forest roof seem now, another lifetime. Faramundo and Ishtar had not chosen the easier part, for their mission was to one despised by the Night, one who dwelt as a count among the Children of Usen.

It was to those between the Carpathian and Apuseni munții that they headed, intending to directly violate the law of non-intervention, a direct challenge to the kingdoms of Necros and of Night. Loving the Light they loved not their lives unto death. Their working plan was to discover the whereabouts of the hidden Count, then to settle down as travellers, integrate with the local population, then cautiously make contact with him. Would he give them a fair hearing, or throw them to the wolves? If he believed their cover story, the former, but if not, the latter was more likely. But they sought to give him a fair chance for the good of their people.

Lilith left them to their fate. Across the waters she flew, soon finding the small hamlet of Lid. It was no use calling to Wulfgar, for after his hammering he would be keeping low, rebuilding his strength. The last person he would expect as friend would be Lilith. She had to painfully trace his movements, for as expected he had crept away from Lid, lest the Night upgrade its punishment to death, and send in assassins to carry out the sentence.

To be lost was to be safe. A weary, scarred looking stranger had been seen heading south. In his condition he probably could not expend his remaining power in swift bat flight, for shapeshifting was not for the weak. As human he would however be able to run day and night without rest. Movement in the dark could expose him to those he would rather avoid. Running in the daylight hours would expose him to curious comment by the secondborn—who ran when they could walk, except for outlaws? She too would move only by daylight, though not for her personal safety but for his. If they knew she was seeking him, his life would be jeopardised and they could find him quicker than she. So it was that she painstakingly traced his steps.

He had been spotted in Nortfigelinge, then Ringeborg, then Tedlagestorp, Harbetorp, Werangle, Bran Cuna, Stinekai, Wacstanest, Castra. Always hugging the coast for around 300 miles. Then someone reported him having headed west—doubling back, going inland? A merry chase. Norwici, Oxenburch, Glinstone, Glenteurde, Jorvalle, to name but a few, west then north.

It seemed to Lilith that Wulfgar had headed back to where he had been, attempting to shake off all traces of his movements. Clever! It was also apparent that he had been stopping in villages or hamlets on bright sunny days, and preferring to set a brisk walking pace in low light conditions, such as woods. It was a case of several months in warm pursuit.

The season of autumn was approaching, and still she had not found Wulfgar. East to Bredlinton—what would later be called Bridlington—which was worth a visit. Situated in the East Riding, it had been hardly worth a mention, but had recently had a priory built by Walter de Grant under Henry 1, which under John was permitted a weekly market—good for revenues—and an annual fair to the Assumption of the Virgin Mary—good for reverence. She was curious to see how the secondborn celebrated such—a curious idea was Mary, and a curious idea was Assumption. Lingering a while might also let her question the attendees about Wulfgar—not but that she was quiet as to his name.

Only as winter was coming on did she at last discover him to be living not too far from a small hamlet called Ghinipe, just a little south of Lid. Curious! When any course of action or inaction could prove fatal, he had marked an exit from Lid. Who would then expect that his exit would eventually be to a place so near, having travelled so far? It came to her mind that she had found more witnesses as to his travel from north to south, as if he had intended that initially his itinerary would clearly show to be eating up the miles going south. Pursuit would travel swiftly past Ghinipe into the south and there get lost, not bothering to recheck the north. Perhaps if pursuit hadn't begun for another year or so or hadn't been so persistent, that plan would have worked, but now she had him cornered, living alone with his back to the sea.

Well almost alone. He had picked up a diminutive friend, who, with his family, lived in what locals called Boggle Holes. But alone to all intent and purposes. These secondborn were small, unimportant, yet vaguely summoned up old memories from another age. Still, she must put them out of her mind and focus on her mission, which consisted of two things. One, bedding down in the North Riding, for she felt that that was somehow Usen's will for her: to live local and to lie low, was his whisper. Two, share the good news with Wulfgar. As to the first thing, if he was settled here she must settle elsewhere, though somewhere quite close, perhaps a little to the north. Anyway, as to... "Wulfgar, greetings. Wait, I mean you no harm." Naturally he had been startled, just rising from the ground as dusk descended, and encountering the Vampire Queen. Who wouldn't be?

"Majesty, what is your pleasure with me?" he asked suspiciously. The queen as assassin was obvious overkill, but why was she there, and who had tracked him to earth?

"Wulfgar, you are behind the times. No longer am I queen; no longer am I of the Night. For I am banished to extraction, of deeper dire than thou, and of my family that was, Ishtar has chosen my way, while Draven is now son of the new queen, Rangda. Of Ishtar, she has other mission, but

I seek thee out." She spoke in terms of familiarity, not of formality, inviting his trust and interest. Not that he could have escaped her, but better not to give heed under anxiety. Her news had to be given, and Wulfgar had to be given quiet space for it to sink in. Calmed, she spoke of Usen, and Hamashiach the Huion. Long did they speak, mind to mind and also, in the way of vampires among non-telepaths, voice to ear, the way of man. They did not enter the boggle holes, but found a nearby copse from where they could see the sea. He listened patiently and politely, with interest but without enthusiasm.

"My queen, for so you remain to me, you who spared herself not in sparing me. For you I am well pleased, for you have peace of mind and are pure of heart. But as for me, you understand not. Beyond hope you offer me freedom, you who have never been bound. Yet I have long abiding guests to whom I am tied, and they to me. Should we depart I fear that I would depart this life, and though you fear not Usen, I sincerely do. My innate strength is but a shade of what it once was, and I dwell in the shade, or in the night. I marvel that you are stronger now, and abide well the light of day, but I fear that beyond death you will but find the damnation that awaits us all imprisoned here from Simboliniad. I cannot deceive myself: his hatred for us is clear. Did he not destroy our world, our joy, lock us into this silent planet and throw away the keys? My guests forbid me to go further. In this I am one with them. My queen, I cannot share your hope."

In vain Lilith reminded him of his mercy to Ulrica: was that not as the opening of the inner prison of the soul, an adumbration of full release available to him? No, he replied, his mercy had been but a weakness, a witness not to his Light but to his decay. "I am a decaying visitor of the Night. How can I spell it out more clearly? What language must I use? I envy your hope, but that hope with disappoint. Yet without hope I can nevertheless live in the light of mercy, as you my queen command. Yet my guests will find this hard to live with, and we will have conflict. Yet they are weak, save in numbers, and in most ways I can still master them. But even if your hope is true, my queen, know now that it was I who killed the last of the unicorn people, my mind sore inflamed by the inner insistence of my guests." There, it was said, and could not be unsaid. That crime had been thoroughly investigated, but the perpetrator had never been brought to justice.

What was that crime? Simbolinians hadn't been the only spirits to emigrate to Earth, though they had been the earliest. Pneumata of another race had arrived late in the day. Also thelodynamics, though of lesser power, they had been welcomed with forbearance as fellow prisoners. They had taken various forms, some fantastical and outré, forms that if you hadn't met them you would think were but mythological beasts. Some were of mixed animal kind, such as centaur and minotaur. Some had become the unctuous unicorns, always keen to please and a legend in battle, now only of legend. They had been of either water or fire clans, and their remains now exist only in sketches by artists of yore. But exist they did.

One by one they perished. Earth was not a good host. Perished most often by the hand of the firstborn, or of the secondborn, by sindeldi or by human, slain needlessly or needfully. One lone unicorn person had sought protection under the Kingdom of Night, one last stallion of stardust. Why should they not accommodate one despised by Usen, who like them had dwelt in deep heaven? The kingdom had been pleased to allow the beast room in a land little populated by mankind, but a major trysting place of the vampires. And so it had grazed in grace, providing the kingdom with a smug sense that it was snubbing its nose at Usen by guarding this lonely beast—a self-satisfying fantasy.

All were under orders to do it no harm, even to offer lite protection, but one day its body had been found dead, butchered, the last of the unicorn race, and the last of those thelodynamics who had unwillingly shared Earth's cell. It had been held a heinous crime against their pride, perhaps done by dunamoi, or perhaps by Usen himself through his aggeloi agents. They wouldn't put it past him to steal in to kill their pet, he who had destroyed their joy. Now at long last it came out: Wulfgar had done it—though not in his right mind— crazed by diaboloi.

Had Lilith known about it at the time, beyond doubt she would have had him slain. But she was now a new Lilith in the age of enlightenment, and now could see that Usen loved, not hated, the Pneumata, thelodynamics from other worlds. His cosmic love offered cosmic forgiveness. Yes, he had forgiven even her. Yet Wulfgar didn't believe, just couldn't believe that. Indeed from what she had just told him, if Usen had loved the unicorn people he would have hated its killer all the more, he told himself. Wulfgar simply could not see how Lilith seemed to ramp up forgiveness all around: no, you love friends, hate enemies; the enemy of your friend is your enemy. Only, he quickly corrected himself, you must have neither friends nor love

Wulfgar would not be swayed, for the time being simply in the Grey Zone. His blood lust he would try to restrain in deference to his queen—though queen of no kingdom even as he was vampire of no kingdom. He would integrate with the fisherfolk of the east, though as a queer sort of chap, not a mixer, but standoffish. She saw that she must be content and wait. She felt a still small voice within her of a time yet to be, a time when Wulfgar would come into the Day when most needed.

"Wulfgar, my friend, it is best that we meet not again save in deep need. Yet it comes to my mind that I should dwell in deep cover in this Riding until some eucatastrophe I see not. A hag and herbal healer I shall be, living but a little distant. As for you, your name you must change, for if the Night seek you, may it not find you? As to the Necros, you are as host and need fear not its wrath. 'My queen' you have called me, and I say to you that on the day that you accept Usen from the heart, on that day you shall be to me a son."

With that promise she left, knowing that Wulfgar would never believe in order to receive, but would receive when he believed. A mercenary belief is hardly worth the name, and no mercenary was he. Her mission now summoned her to nearby Streonshalh, and there she settled down in Florun and waited, but the end—if end there be— was not yet.

THE END? NEVER!

Cosmology

Being Types

- **Powers** (Type 2 beings)—spirits created within the Dynamic Bubble: unfallen Powers were Philikoi; fallen Powers were Turannoi. Three ranks/levels: Cosmic—could oversee a planet; Kingdom (unfallen guardians and fallen dunamoi)—spec ops or province based; Channels/Agents—tertiary helpers, foot soldiers, aggeloi (unfallen) and diaboloi (fallen).

- **Pneumata** (Type 3 beings)—cosmic-born spirits, created outside the Dynamic Bubble. Some were as powerful as Kingdom Powers. Disobedience diminished their power.

- **Psuchai** (Type 4 beings)—global-born spirits, such as sindeldi and humans.

The Pantocrator created Powers, Pneumata, and Psuchai, which could fall into disobedience. Powers outside the Dynamic Bubble could not change, but the hidden rebellion or submission of a few—systemic or superficial—could surface in real time. Phusika (Type 5 or lesser beings) he also created through intelligent code, but not in his Image. But to those of mortal souls, he gave images, dreams.

Spirit Kingdom Types

- **Necros**: actively against creator and creation
- **Night**: actively against creator
- **Grey Zone**: betwixt kingdoms, passively towards creator and creation, uncommitted
- **Dawn**: actively towards creator and creation
- **Day**: Hamashiachim actively towards creator and creation

The **Necros** is dark in heart and mind; the **Night** is dark in mind: in general terms, both are of the **Dark**. The **Dawn** is light in heart; the **Day** is light in heart and mind: in general terms, both are of the **Light**. The **Grey**, unsure and unaligned, is unconsciously of the **Light**.

Primary Characters

Draven: Type 3 (Dark) / Royal

Grindan: Type 3 (Dark) / Killed

Hamashiach (Huion): Type 4 (Light) / Sui Generis

Ishtar/Inanna: Type 3 (Dark to Light) / Adopted sister to Ereshkigal, shadowminder

Kendra/Docina: Type 3 (Dark)

Lilith/Kiskilla: Type 3 (Dark to Light) / Adopted daughter to Meslamtæa / extracted

Marwolaeth/Maudlin: Type 3 (Dark) / Family Mother

Necuratu: Type 2 (Dark) / Dark Lord

Nindara: Type 3 (Dark) / Royal

Rangda/Calon Arang: Type 3 (Dark) / Royal

Usen Pantocrator (Deo): Type 1 (The Light) / Cosmic Creator

Wulfgar/Lorell: Type 3 (Dark to Grey) / Extracted

Books by this author

Theology

Israel's Gone Global

Israel's Gone Global traces salvation through the term, Israel. Was the covenant with the people-nation of Yakob-Yisrael, crossed out? How eternal is covenant? To examine that, we examine marriage. Can a covenant partner be truly divorced? Has Yeshua-Yisrael mediated a spiritual covenant with a spiritual Israel? Is evangelism of ethnic Jews needless, a priority, or neither?

No one could have everlasting life but for the cross, but has it always been globally accessible? Might any who die as Atheists, Hindus, or Islamists, make heaven? And is eternal life joyful? Is everlasting life fun?

Tackling the question of people who die in infancy (or as adults who never heard the gospel), we consider whether it is fair if only those who don't die in infancy get a chance of eternal damnation (if infant universalism), or alone get a chance of eternal heaven (if infant damnation). Does predilectionism make best sense of biblical revelation?

Opportunities to enjoy eternal life spring from the new covenant—reasons to rejoice. But what about salvation history before that covenant?

∞

Singing's Gone Global

Singing's Gone Global, briefly explores the background of singing, before and into ancient Israel. It examines the impact songs have on those who sing, and on those who listen, touching on spiritual warfare. It looks at how nonsense songs neither make sense to evangelism, nor to the evangelised, and asks, "Is there a mûmak in the room?"

Oddly some songwriters simply misunderstand prayer. Part two covers the basics of the trinity, focusing on the spirit in order to understand types of prayer (eg request, gratitude, adoration, chat), leading in turn to a better understanding of our heavenly father, our brother, our helper, and ourselves in Christ's likeness.

Next we look at some common problems. Part three focuses on problems such as buddyism, decontextualising, misvisualisation, and unitarianism. Diagnosis can help Christ's 'bride' to recover from suboptimal and unbiblical songs (Eph.5:18-30).

Giving a Problem Avoidance Grade (PAG)—an A+ to Unsatisfactory scale—in part four we examine specific songs. Weapons forged (Part three), the mûmakil can be attacked, seeking to save and be saved.

Subsequently the book concludes by showing how Christmas carols may be tweaked to better serve our weary world, rejoicing that joy to the world has come.

∞

The Word's Gone Global

The Word's Gone Global, examines Bible text (trusted by early Islam) and introduces textual critique. It looks at the Eastern Orthodox Bible and the Latin Vulgate. Did the Reformation improve text and translation? Were Wycliffe, Tyndale, and Martin, helpful?

Why did the New International Version begin, and why does it enrage? Why did complementarians Don Carson and Wayne Grudem, clash? Is marketing hype between formal and functional equivalence, meaningless? Which version or versions should you regularly read?

In English-speaking circles, Broughton wished to burn Bancroft's King James Version, yet many KJV proponents—think Gail Riplinger and Peter Ruckman—wish to burn all alternatives. More heat than light?

Grade Charts cover 30+ English versions on issues such as God's name, God's son's deity, marriage, gender terms, anti-polytheism, and various issues in John's Gospel. No, Tyndale was not 'born again'. No, John was not antisemitic. No, he did not disagree with the other Gospels.

∞

Prayer's Gone Global

Prayer's Gone Global, begins with ancient civilisations and prayer (the Common Level). Then it narrows into Ancient Israel and prayer (the Sinai Level). Then it deepens and widens into Global Israel and prayer (the Christian Level). Deity is revealed as trinity: Sabellians mislead.

Relating to the trinity includes the Holy Spirit. We should of course work with him, but should we worship him, complain to him, chat with him? Above the spirit stands the often forgotten father—oh let Jesusism retire.

Authority is another issue. Are we authorised to decree and declare? Is binding and loosing actually prayer, or is it evangelism? Is it biblical never to command miracles? Do we miss out on the supernatural which Jesus modelled for us, too fearful of strange fire to offer holy fire?

You can freshen up your prayer life—ride the blessed camel, not the gnats. Listen to Saint Anselm pray, and C S Lewis and 'Malcolm' discuss prayer, and be blessed.

∞

Revelation's Gone Global

Revelation's Gone Global, is a telling of John's future, as if by a then contemporary named Sonafets speaking to his church about how John's apocalyptic scroll related to their days, and about what was still future to John.

Encouragement is a big theme. Roman persecution was an unpredictable beast which ferociously lashed out here and there—what church or Christian was safe? But God stood behind the scenes, allowing but limiting their enemy, and messiah walked among the churches, lights to the world.

Victory lay neither with Rome nor demons, but with God, and with the warrior lamb who had been slain. Victory was guaranteed, and would finally be enjoyed.

Exhortation was given to believers, to play their part while on the mortal stage. They were to walk in the light, and not to let the show down by straying.

Angels of power, actively working out God's will, far exceed the puny forces against God and his church. His wrath was not pleasant, but could be redemptive until the new age begins.

C S Lewis' essay, The World's Last Night, is briefly examined to enjoin a calm awareness of the ongoing battle we are in, and the brightness to come when the king returns.

∞

The Father's Gone Global

Focusing from God as father, to the specific person of God the father, The Father's Gone Global looks at the biblical parent/child pattern from Genesis, through Sinai, and into the Church.

Abba as a new covenant word expresses deep filial affection even under deep anguish in our Gethsemane battles. Coming through God's belovèd son, it speaks into the church and into our lives.

Though to many the 'forgotten father', human parents/fathers should 'put on' God the father, and his children should 'put on' his son. We forget him to our cost.

Human applications aside, what is the Eternal Society? Is filial relationship modelled by God the son incarnate? Are we to be always obedient to our father and guided by the spirit?

Eschatologically the father will be supreme, but even now he is the one to whom the son points. Christian life should relate to God our father, God our brother, and God our helper, prioritising the father.

Renewal of the church is vital for our confused world, but renewal which downplays the father falls short of the good news which Christ created and the spirit circulates. May this book play its part.

∞

Salvation Now and Life Beyond

Salvation Now, divides the doctrine of salvation into the four main levels of common humanity, the old covenant, the new covenant, and life beyond.

A big weight is put on the term, Israel, as God's master plan. This too has four levels, meaning a man, a people, a new man, and a new people, respectively.

Various ideas of what Christianity, the new covenant for the new people, is good for, and how we get into it and best enjoy it, are examined, and a faith-based inexclusivism is suggested.

Everlasting life is seen as the ultimate goal of salvation, universal meaningfulness and love beyond all fears and pains.

∞

Revisiting

Revisiting The Challenging Counterfeit

Revisiting The Challenging Counterfeit, is an extended review of Raphael Gasson's 'The Challenging Counterfeit' (1966). Raphael was an ethnic Jew whose spiritual journey included many years as a Christian Spiritualist minister.

Today, when psychic phenomena captures the imagination and the bank accounts of popular media, it is useful to unearth the witness of one who had well worn the T-shirt of a medium with pride, only to bury it in unholy ground as a thing of shame and of sorrow and of wasted time.

Challengingly, his book exposes what true Spiritualism is. He had nothing but high praise for Spiritualists, and deep condemnation for Spiritualism. For he had discovered true Spiritualism to be itself a fake of true Spirituality, a mere Counterfeit that, in deposing death in the mind, enthroned it in the soul.

Counterfeit phenomena covered include apparitions, Rescue Work and haunted houses, materialisation of pets, psychic healing, Lyceums, clairvoyance, and OOBEs—to name but a few. This book surveys his exposé of Spiritualism's offer of fascinating fish bait, false food falling short of real food for the soul. Though it takes issue with

Raphael on a number of points, his core insights are powerful and timely, helping us to avoid—or escape from—a Challenging Counterfeit, and to discover true spiritual currency.

∞

Revisiting The Pilgrim's Progress

Revisiting The Pilgrim's Progress, is a re-dreaming of John Bunyan's most famous dream. An ex-serviceman and ex-jailbird, he found fortune, freedom, and fans worldwide.

This dream journey is substantially Bunyan's from this world, and into that which is to come. It is not a fun story, but it has lots of danger, and joy, and reflection on some big life themes.

Profoundly, sinners who become pilgrims become saints. But that can make life more difficult. One big question is, Is it worth it? One big temptation is, Turn back or turn aside. And if you see others do so, that makes it harder not to. Bunyan was tempted. And he discovered that not deserting, can lead to despair. But he also discovered a key to liberty.

Pre-eminently, it is a story of grace which many follow. Grace begins the journey, helps along the way, and brings the story to a happily ever after. Are all fairy stories based on heaven?

∞

Fantasy

The Simbolinian Files

From Simboliniad, a crystal planet long gone, came the vampire race, the wapierze, thelodynamic shapeshifters seeking blood. Most oppose Usen, King of the Light, so side with the Necros. Seldom do the Guardians intervene. These files, secretly secured from various insider sources, reveal something of what they have done, and will do.

∞

Vampire Redemption

Artificial intelligence, created by superpowers to save man, questions man's worth, and becomes The Beast. Escaping into the wild, many discover a wilderness infested by zombies and diabolical spirits. Who will help? Father Doyle? He's tied up with the mysterious Lilith.

Tariq? He's tied up with Wilma. Can the bigoted old exorcist deliver him from evil?

Radical problems can require radical solutions. But does man really need hobs, elves, and the more ancient of days? In the surrounding shadows, vampires and demons form an alliance, raising the stakes against Whitby and Tyneside. Powerful vampires live shrouded within Whitby, speaking of life beyond this galaxy. Is salvation in the stars? Is Sunniva, the despised woman of Alban, worth dying for? Big questions, needing big answers. Not even Guardian Odin can foretell man's fate and, as silent stars go by, one little town must awake from its dreams.

Though The Beast slumbers purposeless and undisturbed, in the far west a global giant slowly opens its yellow eyes and threatens to smother the earth in fire and ice. There is one chance only.

∞

Vampire Extraction

Bitterly long their imprisoned spirits lay, fast bound to Earth's drowsy decay. To the Simbolinian race, there was no hell on Earth, for Earth was hell, and Usen the cosmic jailer. Was it so surprising that as vampires they stalked Usen's children for blood? Most chose the Kingdom of Night, wary of both the Kingdom of Necros and the Kingdom of Dawn.

As queen of the Night, Lilith's story streams through the summer sands of Sumer, and through the green woods of Sherwood. It flags up both dishonour and joy, and cuts across the paths of Ulrica the Saxon and Robin the Hood, as tyrannies rise and fall in merry England. Bigotry seldom has a good word to say about Usen, nor about mercy. Reluctantly, Lilith examines what it means to show mercy, to show weakness. Wulfgar had enslaved Ulrica: is it mercy to let her burn; should mercy have spared Lona? Could Hamashiach turn daughter into sister? Could Count Dracula be turned from his madness? Has Draven really betrayed his mother? Life has many questions.

Tales picture ideas, letting us walk through the eyes of others to better see ourselves. This story exposes subplots behind common history. How these chronicles came to be written up is, in the spirit confidentiality, not for the public eye. What truth is within you must judge. Discrimination is a gift from Beyond, from which the words still echo: mercy is better than sacrifice. Indeed mercy can be sacrifice. Judge well.

∞

Vampire Count

Vampires were not always earthbound, nor are all evil, but being victims of Usen's Eighth Law, his Children became their fair game. Yet the Night Kingdom was divided: some veered to the Necros; some to the Dawn. Who was wrong; who was right?

Long ago one incited his people to racial violence against elven and human kinds. Ever he strove to be king of the Night, and unto Necuratu the Dark Lord he gave the dragon shape. He made war upon the ancient Middle East, even the Nephilim War. Against him the Light raised flood and division.

At last his own people, paying the price of his rampage, bound him in deep sleep. Yet the millennia seemed meaningless to him: even the rising of Hamashiach hardly disturbed his dreams. At last awoken, he and his brides stalked the hills of Transylvania. Only the fear of Lilith—and after her unforgivable sin, Queen Rangda—chained their bloodlust.

Dracula sought escape and autonomy. By cunning and devious means, he immigrated to London via Whitby. Pursuit followed swiftly, with a shadowminder helping a circle of human headhunters, though they sought the death of all vampires.

∞

Vampire Grail

Wulfgar is a vampire, a thelodynamic creature from another galaxy, now locked into our world by one called the Cosmic Jailer. He hides a tormenting secret from his queen, Lilith, which the Necros use as blackmail. She will only go so far with the Necros against Hamashiach—Wulfgar must go further.

Unknown to the Darkness, to bury Hamashiach is to plant the Light. From the buried seed springs life, and humanity must reimagine itself. Longinus turns to The Way, the nexus of the Seventh Age. His spear goes on a special mission to the island of Briton, where Wulfgar lives again.

Logres is centred on Avalon, but raises up Arthur, a man of mixed race, to carry its flag and to protect against the Saxons. But its main enemy is the Darkness, which ever seeks to extinguish the Light it hates and fears.

Finally, it seems as if the Darkness has won, and the dark ages descend. But does the Light not shine in the Darkness? Must Wulfgar remain in the Night?

∞

Vampire Shadows

Dark vampires, hidden within the ancient empire of Khem, fall out with the king who, stirred up by the Necros, enslaves the Sheep People. But Iahveh, the shepherd-divinity, is stirred up, and stirs up a hidden hero to force a way out.

Apprehensively the two vampire-magicians join the Sheep of Iahveh, on their long and deadly trek in search of a promised land. Can any survive?

Warily they ask deep questions. Is Usen evil, as prejudice says? Is he possibly a good jailer? Are his unusual regulations, meaningful? They risk ending up in death.

Neverendingly the Sheep's sorry story drags out in interminable peregrination. Weary of wandering, most would settle for some green pastures and untroubled waters. But as they well know, that would take a miracle.

Notes

i   Among the divinities, alliances could be known by familial terms such as husband/wife/son/aunt. In some kingdoms alliance changes (like job placements) were frequent, so a mother's son one year could be her father the next. The nearest to biological birth—parenthood—was occasionally other spirits summoned forth from the Dynamic Bubble.

ii   Diaboloi, both feminine and masculine (not biological females and males), infest our world. The Guardians include feminine and masculine, although at the tertiary level Earth based aggeloi are only masculine foot soldiers.

www.ingramcontent.com/pod-product-compliance
Lightning Source LLC
Chambersburg PA
CBHW030614130626
46552CB00002B/553